Charise Mericle Harper

SASQUATCH AND ALIENS

BOOK ONE

ALIEN ENCOUNTER

Christy Ottaviano Books

Henry Holt and Company

NEW YORK

For all who believe in the unseen—
it makes life more interesting!

Henry Holt and Company, LLC
Publishers since 1866
175 Fifth Avenue
New York, New York 10010
mackids.com

Henry Holt® is a registered trademark of Henry Holt and Company, LLC.

Library of Congress Cataloging-in-Publication Data
Harper, Charise Mericle, author, illustrator.
Alien encounter / Charise Mericle Harper.
    pages   cm. – (Sasquatch and aliens ; 1)
Summary: Nine-year-old Morgan of the Pacific Northwest is fascinated with aliens and the
sasquatch, but his real adventures begin when he meets Lewis, whose parents just bought a
motel named the Stay On Inn.
ISBN 978-0-8050-9621-7 (hardback)
[1. Friendship–Fiction. 2. Family life–Northwest, Pacific–Fiction. 3. Extraterrestrial beings–
Fiction. 4. Yeti–Fiction. 5. Northwest, Pacific–Fiction. 6. Humorous stories.] I. Title.
PZ7.H231323Ali 2014   [Fic]–dc23   2013039906

Henry Holt books may be purchased for business or promotional use.
For information on bulk purchases, please contact Macmillan Corporate and Premium Sales
Department at (800) 221-7945 x5442 or by e-mail at specialmarkets@macmillan.com.

First Edition—2014 / Designed by April Ward

Printed in the United States of America by
R. R. Donnelley & Sons Company, Harrisonburg, Virginia

1 3 5 7 9 10 8 6 4 2

An Acrostic Poem About Lewis

LIVES IN A MOTEL.

EATS STRANGE FOODS.

WILL DO ALMOST ANYTHING.

IS NEW IN TOWN.

SLEEPS UNDER A PAIR OF RIPPED UNDERPANTS.

Why I Met Lewis

I met Lewis because of underpants. This is not a normal way to meet someone. When weird things happen, they are usually a surprise.

KINDS OF UNDERPANTS

PLAIN
BOXERS

BOXERS
WITH
PATTERN

PLAIN
WHITE
UNDERPANTS

↑

LEWIS'S
KIND

UNDERPANTS
WITH A
PATTERN

The Woods

Lewis and I met in the woods. I don't know what he was doing, but I was there looking for a stick. It was for my new invention—the triple slingshot. Slingshots are easy to make. The only hard part is finding the right stick, and if you need lots of sticks to choose from, the woods are the perfect place to look. They're filled with sticks. If I'd been looking for a regular stick, I probably would have been done in about two seconds, but I wasn't. Special sticks take a lot longer to find.

THE SPECIAL STICK

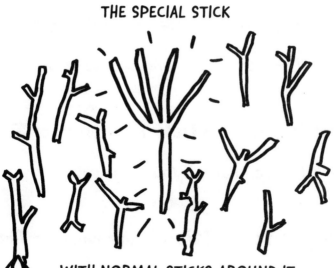

WITH NORMAL STICKS AROUND IT

An Acrostic About What I Will Make with the Perfect Stick

SUPER SLINGSHOT.

TRIPLE FIRING POWER.

IT NEVER MISSES.

CAN HIT THREE TARGETS AT ONCE.

KING OF THE SLINGSHOTS.

3

Looking for a **Stick** (Hour Number One)

I bet I'll find that stick any minute now.

Looking for a **Stick** (Hour Number Two)

I can't believe I haven't found the stick yet.

Looking for a **Stick** (Hour Number Three)

Stupid impossible-to-find stick!

It's not easy to think good thoughts when you've been disappointed for almost 10,800 seconds in a row. That's probably why I suddenly remembered Dad's saying.

DAD LOOKING HAPPY WHILE HE SAYS SOMETHING
THAT MAKES THE PERSON HE IS TALKING TO SAD.

JUST BECAUSE YOU WANT SOMETHING DOESN'T MEAN YOU'RE GOING TO GET IT.

Sometimes it's hard to tell if the stuff Dad says is true or not. He tells jokes without laughing, and says real things while smiling. He's a confusing guy. Even though I didn't want to believe him, my brain was starting to think that maybe his saying was true. Maybe I wouldn't find my stick or, worse, maybe it didn't even exist.

THINGS THAT DO NOT EXIST

TIME MACHINES

SUPERPOWERS

MY STICK

The One Thing You Should Be Scared of if You Hear It in the Woods

SCREAMING!

If you are in the woods and you hear screaming, your first thought should be **DANGER!**

A good idea for a second thought would be **BEAR ATTACK!**

BAD IDEAS FOR A SECOND THOUGHT

NAP TIME	TOILET TIME	DANCE TIME
TACO TIME	JUMPING JACK TIME	SINGING TIME

I don't know if Twin Rivers has ever had a real bear attack, but last year we had an almost bear attack. My across-the-street neighbor Mrs. Lee saw a bear in her backyard. He could have eaten her, except she was inside getting some iced tea to drink with her lunch.

She said, "Iced tea saved my life!"

Our whole town knew about it because she got to be on TV, and every time the camera did a close-up, she said the exact same thing. "Iced tea saved my life!" She probably said it more than twenty times.

Mrs. Lee said she was filling her glass with iced tea when she looked out her window and saw a big, furry thing sitting at her picnic table. It was a bear, and he was eating her lunch. He ate her tuna sandwich, her strawberries, and even her broccoli salad (he must have been really hungry to eat that).

She took a ton of pictures. One of them even got in the paper. It was a picture of the bear at the table with the sandwich in his paws. He was sitting up and looked just like a person, except he was furry, had huge claws and teeth, and could totally kill you.

BEAR

TUNA SANDWICH
STRAWBERRIES
BROCCOLI SALAD
(YUCK!)

Everyone at school was super excited about the bear, until Marcus Wolver kind of ruined it. He made up a fake rumor. Most people didn't believe him, but a few did, and that was annoying because now instead of everyone being excited, some people were grumpy about the Lees.

IT WAS JUST MR. LEE WEARING A BEAR SUIT!

NINCOMPOOP

The Thing That Is Wrong with Marcus

Marcus is a nincompoop.

Normally, I wouldn't pick a dumb word like that, but Mom said I'm not even allowed to think about the other word I wanted to use. She's pretty bossy about stuff like that. She says old-fashioned words are more polite, but that's probably just because no one knows what they mean.

YOUNG PERSON

I made up an acrostic to help describe Marcus and the word *nincompoop*—I think it helps.

MOSTLY IS ANNOYING.

ALWAYS TRIES TO STEAL JUICE BOXES AT LUNCHTIME.

REALLY THINKS HE IS AWESOME.

CAN ARGUE ABOUT ANYTHING.

UH . . . WHAT HE SAYS WHENEVER A TEACHER ASKS HIM A QUESTION.

SPITS WHILE HE TALKS . . . ON PURPOSE!

Marcus was wrong about the Lees for a lot of reasons, but the main reason he was wrong was that he didn't know them. This is important because if he knew them, he'd know that the Lees are not costume-loving people, and people who do not like costumes do not run around in bear suits.

I know this because the Lees are my neighbors, and even if you don't want to, you learn stuff about people when they live right across the street from you.

Things I Know About the Lees

- Mr. Lee spends a lot of time working in his garage.
- Mrs. Lee likes to garden.
- Mr. Lee fixes furniture for a job.
- The Lees hate Halloween—every Halloween they turn off their lights so it looks like they're not home.

WHAT YOU SHOULD DO IF YOU ARE PRETENDING NOT TO BE HOME

MOVE YOUR CAR OUT OF YOUR DRIVEWAY.

My sister, Betty, says they do that because they're cheapos and don't want to give out candy, but Mom says that's probably wrong. She thinks they are just tired from a long day of work and don't want to have to get up every two seconds to answer the door. I believe Mom because even though Betty is twelve and I'm nine that doesn't mean she is smarter than me. She is wrong about a lot of things.

THINGS MY ANNOYING SISTER HAS BEEN WRONG ABOUT

Proof That the Lees Are Not Cheapos

Every Christmas the Lees give us a giant tin full of pretzels and three kinds of popcorn (the chocolate popcorn is the best). This is not a cheapo present. A cheapo present would be the smallest tin, the one that comes with only the regular popcorn.

I told this to Betty, but she said, "What? I don't care about that anymore." She has the attention span of a hamster.

CHEAPO · LESS CHEAPO · PROBABLY NOT CHEAPO · NO WAY CHEAPO

THE ONE WE GET

Sometimes if you know something and other people say you're wrong, you just have to ignore them and keep on believing it. That's how I feel about Mr. Lee—no matter what anyone says, I think he's OK.

TWO THINGS ABOUT MR. LEE THAT DO NOT GO WITH WEARING A BEAR SUIT

MR. LEE **ALWAYS** WEARS HIS HAT.

HE WALKS WITH A CANE, THOUGH HE DOESN'T SEEM LIKE HE REALLY NEEDS IT. HE MOVES PRETTY FAST!

What Happened to the Bear After It Ate Mrs. Lee's Lunch?

It walked away.

What Happened to the People After the Bear Ate Mrs. Lee's Lunch?

They got scared. Some got crazy scared, like Carla Minkel, a girl in my class. She said that even though tuna sandwiches were her favorite sandwiches in the whole world, she was never going to eat another one for as long as she lived.

She said, "I don't want to be a bear magnet."

Mom and Dad were pretty scared too because they gave me a whistle and said, "You have to promise to carry this with you at all times!"

Dad said, "If you're in the woods and get into trouble, blow the whistle, and I'll come and save you."

I didn't say anything, but my imagination dressed him up like a superhero. He looked ridiculous!

Mom saw me smiling and got mad.

DAD AS A SUPERHERO

MASK FROM THE DRESS-UP BOX

PLAIN SHIRT WITH D WRITTEN IN MARKER

HIS OLD SWIMSUIT FROM WHEN HE WENT TO COLLEGE

MOM'S TIGHTS THAT ARE TOO SHORT

HAIRY LEGS

HIS HIKING BOOTS THAT HE GOT ON SALE—THEY ARE WEIRD-LOOKING

It was too hard to explain what I was thinking about, so I just apologized instead. Sometimes that's easier than a big explanation.

I put my head down and said, "Sorry for laughing."

Betty's foot was peeking out from the corner in the hall, so I knew she was listening. She loves it when I get in trouble. I'm sure she was smiling!

I had to tell Mom "I promise I will always carry the whistle" about twenty times before she finally believed me.

It was an easy promise to make—nobody wants to be a bear snack, and the whistle was pretty small. But that was months ago, and right now I had a bigger problem. I was in the woods and someone had just screamed. Even someone like Marcus Wolver would know what that meant. Screaming always means **DANGER!**

What I Did the Second After I Heard the Screaming in the Woods

I grabbed my whistle and started blowing it like crazy. It's good that I had something to do, or I probably would have been screaming, or maybe something worse. While I was blowing, I looked around for the bear, but I couldn't see anything except trees and bushes. And all I could hear was the whistle and my super-loud breaths in between blowing. It was the kind of thing that can totally freak you out!

ME FREAKING OUT AND BLOWING THE WHISTLE— BOTH AT ONCE

My List of Didn'ts

- I *didn't* see a bear.
- I *didn't* get eaten by a bear.
- Dad *didn't* come and save me.

For sure I was going to tell Dad that his Save Me Whistle Plan was a . . .

TOTAL FAIL!

What Can Happen After You Blow a Whistle for Ten Minutes and Nothing Happens

You decide to stop blowing. This is a good thing because blowing a whistle for a really long time is not easy—it messes with your brain. My head felt like a giant balloon, and even though I wasn't blowing anymore, I could still hear the whistle sound in my ears.

I was sitting down to rest when someone shouted, **"DON'T BLOW THAT WHISTLE!"**

I screamed, jumped back up, and dropped the whistle.

I was scared, but it was in a new way, not the bear way.

"UP HERE! UP HERE!" shouted the voice.

I looked around to find where the voice was coming from. It was somewhere above me. And then high in the branches of a tree, I saw him—a boy waving at me.

What Surprise Looks Like

When your brain is surprised, sometimes you can't help but open your mouth. This is an OK thing to do if you are in a house, but not such a good idea if you are outside in the woods. The woods are filled with bugs.

WHY BEING SURPRISED OUTSIDE
CAN BE A BAD THING

1 SURPRISE LOOK WITH THREE BUGS FLYING AROUND

2 SURPRISE LOOK WITH BUG IN THE MOUTH

3 SURPRISE LOOK WITH BUG IN THE THROAT AND TONGUE STICKING OUT

I spit, I gagged, I coughed, and still the bug was stuck. By the time it was in my throat, it was too late. I couldn't stop it—my body swallowed!

The boy in the tree was laughing, but I was in bug shock and still worried about the bear, so I ignored him. Finally, after a few more minutes of nothing bad happening, I looked back up at him.

"Why are you up there?" I shouted. "Did you see a bear?"

"No bear," he shouted. "I'm stuck. I can't get down. Look!"

He wiggled his arms and legs around to show me. Something about him looked strange. A minute later, I figured it out. He wasn't holding on to anything—his arms and legs were completely free. He wiggled them around like a giant beetle. I couldn't see what it was, but something behind him was holding him up.

NORMAL BEETLE

BEETLE STUCK ON HIS BACK

I'VE GOT TO WIGGLE MY LEGS SO I CAN TURN OVER.

TREE

WHAT A BEETLE WOULD LOOK LIKE STUCK IN A TREE

"HEY!" shouted the boy. "What's your name?"

"Morgan Hen—" I answered, but I stopped myself before adding the rest. This wasn't school.

WHAT YOU SAY AT SCHOOL WHEN YOU GIVE YOUR NAME

What Happened Next?

"MORGAN! Hey, Morgan," the boy was shouting again.

I looked up.

"Come up here and help me."

I nodded, picked up my whistle, and walked to the base of the tree. He was lucky I was a good climber—in about ten seconds, I was standing on a branch next to him. Before I could say anything, or even understand why he was stuck, he smiled and pointed to the back of his pants.

"I'm Lewis," he said. "And I have a giant wedgie!"

Can a Tree Give You a Giant Wedgie?

YES! Yes, it can! I was wishing I was like Mrs. Lee and had a camera with me because some things you just have to take a picture of . . . or no one will ever believe you.

What You Should Definitely Ask When You See a Tree Wedgie

"HOW DID YOU DO THAT?"

I pointed to the wedgie and burst out laughing.

For a second, Lewis didn't say anything, but then he threw his arms in the air and said, "I know! Awesome, right?" He flapped his arms and kicked his legs like he was swimming.

It was one of those things I would have never believed unless I'd seen it, and here I was seeing it with my very own eyes!

Lewis squirmed some more and made a crazy face. I grabbed the branch above me with two hands and held on tight. Laughing really hard, high up in a tree, is not safe.

TREE SAFETY

BEING STILL IS SAFE.

MOVING AROUND IS NOT SAFE.

After a while, we got too tired to laugh anymore. This can happen, but only if something is super funny.

Helping Lewis

"That's a killer wedgie," I said. I inspected the stick. It had poked a hole right through the back of Lewis's underpants. He was definitely stuck.

"Push up with your feet and then maybe you can slide off," I suggested.

He scowled. "I can't push up! Don't you think I'd push up if I could push up? YOU have to help me!"

I looked at his feet. He was right. I hadn't noticed it before, but there weren't any branches near them. There was absolutely nothing for him to push up from. His feet were just dangling in space.

"You have to pull me up," said Lewis. He lifted his arms so I could grab them. I tried, but there was no way I could do it. He was too heavy.

I slumped back against my branch, out of breath. I shook my head. "It's impossible."

"Well, I can't stay here!" said Lewis. "Maybe I can break the stick." He started squirming.

He shook back and forth, but it was useless — the stick wasn't going to break. The tree was too strong.

My Idea That Lewis Did Not Like

"You wait here, and I'll go get help," I said. It was the only thing I could think of.

"Wait," said Lewis. "How do I know you'll come

back? Maybe you'll forget about me. Or forget which tree I'm in."

I thought for a moment. He had a point. All the trees looked pretty much the same. But then . . .

"Here." I pulled the whistle out of my pocket. "If you blow this, I'll hear it, and then I'll find you. Plus you're really good at screaming."

Suddenly I remembered how scared I'd been. I leaned on my branch and studied Lewis. I had a few questions.

"Why did you scream when you saw me? Why didn't you just yell out **HELP** or **LOOK HERE**?"

Lewis smiled and shook his head like he couldn't believe I had to ask. "Screams are louder than yells," he said. "Everybody knows that."

While I was thinking about that, he pointed to my pocket.

"What else do you have?" he asked. "I need something more special. Something you'll for sure come back to get. This whistle doesn't seem very important."

I felt around in my pocket and shrugged. "I don't know. Just normal stuff." I emptied my pocket into my hands and held them out. There wasn't much to choose from, just a bottle cap, the key for my back door, my pocketknife, my whistle, and some coins.

Slowly Lewis nodded and smiled. It made me wonder what he was going to pick.

WHAT WAS IN MY POCKET

Lewis's Idea That I Did Not Like

Lewis pointed to the pocketknife. "**PERFECT!**" he shouted. "You can free me! You can cut my underpants!"

"**WHAT? NO WAY!** I'm not touching them!" I put everything back in my pocket and shoved the pocketknife toward him. "Here, you take it!"

There was no way I was going to touch his underpants!

Lewis took the knife and opened it. He twisted around right, twisted around left, but neither way was good. His arms couldn't reach far enough behind him. He couldn't cut himself free. After about five minutes of trying, he finally gave up.

Lewis looked over at me and held out the knife. He didn't say a word. He didn't have to. I knew what was next. Either I had to help him or I had to leave him hanging. It was a hard decision.

What Is Not Easy to Do?

To cut whatever underpants are made of with a pocketknife is not easy for a lot of reasons.

Why I Helped Lewis

I don't know why I helped Lewis. Sometimes you just do stuff without really knowing why you made that choice. This was one of those times.

The List of Promises

Before I started, I made Lewis say a whole list of promises. This was a safe thing to do because sometimes the world doesn't need to know everything.

SOMETIMES THE WORLD CAN BE MEAN

I'M GOING TO HAVE FUN MAKING FUN OF YOU.

PROMISES THAT LEWIS MADE TO ME OUT LOUD, IN NATURE, SO HE BETTER KEEP THEM

① I promise not to make fun of Morgan for touching my underpants—even if it was only the top part of the very back.

② I promise to never tell anyone that Morgan touched my underpants—even if it was only the top part of the very back.

If someone asks me if Morgan touched my underpants,
I will lie and say no. I will even lie to my mom. But if
she is dying, then I can tell her the truth.

 If someone asks how I got out of the tree wedgie,
I will say I cut my own underpants.

 Even if Morgan and I are enemies, I will never tell
about the underpants.

Gravity Is an Important Thing to Remember

Lewis and I did not think about gravity. It was bad
planning. Gravity was the reason Lewis crashed
down out of the tree the second his underpants
were free. I didn't hear a thump, but there must
have been one, because when I looked down, he
was on the ground on his back.

The Good Thing About the Fall

Most falls are not good, unless you start thinking
about what could have gone worse but didn't. If
the list of things that didn't happen gets long

enough, your brain can suddenly start to think, "Hey, that was a pretty good fall."

I watched Lewis roll around on the ground. He was moving. He wasn't dead. That was number one on my list.

As I climbed down after him, my list got longer and longer.

MY GOOD FALL LIST

① NOT DEAD.

② NOT BLEEDING LIKE A FOUNTAIN.

③ NOT CHOKING.

④ NOT PARALYZED.

⑤ NO BONES STICKING OUT OF SKIN.

What Lewis Said That Was a Surprise

When I got to the ground, Lewis was sitting up, looking at his leg. It was bleeding, and it looked bad. I couldn't see the cut, but there was blood. Lewis was in the middle of tying his long-sleeve T-shirt around his leg. How did he know to do that? Probably a Boy Scout thing, I guessed. When he was done, he looked up and half grinned.

"You know what that was?" he asked.

I shook my head.

"Amazing!" he said. "Maybe the most amazing thing that's ever happened to me!" And then for a second, he was quiet. "I never want to forget it," he said.

I nodded like I was agreeing with him, but my brain was thinking other things.

But I had to be nice—Lewis was hurt. Maybe the crazy talk wasn't his fault. Maybe he'd hit his head on the way down. I looked at his head. It looked fine. No bumps or bruises or blood—at least not that I could see.

"Do you have a camera?" asked Lewis. "So we can remember the exact tree and where we were sitting."

He pointed up. I shook my head.

"I want to come back later and look at it," he said. "It's important!"

I looked down at his leg. The blood was seeping through the T-shirt. That looked more important. We had to get out of there. He needed a doctor.

"We should just go," I said. I moved forward to help him up, but Lewis shifted away from me.

"I'm not leaving until we mark the tree!" He glared at me and crossed his arms.

Fine, if he wanted me to mark the tree, then I'd do it—anything so we could leave. I'd never been with a dead person before, and I didn't want Lewis to be my first.

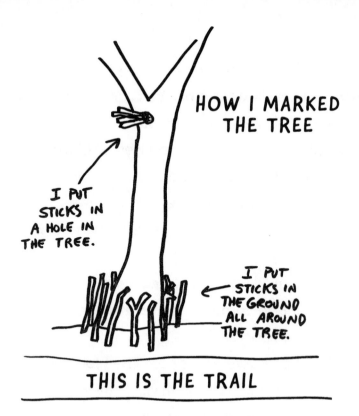

HOW I MARKED THE TREE

I PUT STICKS IN A HOLE IN THE TREE.

I PUT STICKS IN THE GROUND ALL AROUND THE TREE.

THIS IS THE TRAIL

Remembering the Tree

Getting Lewis to stand up was pretty easy, but moving forward was harder. It was weird—his bleeding leg was OK to stand on, but his other leg, the one that looked perfectly normal, was not.

I found a long stick for him to use as a crutch, and then held his arm on the other side. At first we were pretty clumsy, but after a couple of minutes, we were walking a lot better.

"It's like a three-legged race," I said. "If we're ever in one, we'll be good, from all this practice."

Lewis winced, but nodded.

Suddenly he stopped moving and looked back down the trail. "What if someone steals the sticks? Then we won't find the tree."

Now I was sure that his brain was scrambled. Who'd steal a bunch of sticks?

Lewis shouted out the answer. "**BEAVERS!**" He stuck out his front teeth, and then snapped them up and down. "Beavers love sticks!"

It would have been funny, except he was still bleeding.

"Beavers live by water," I said. "And there's no water here. Plus they use special sticks, not the kind I used around the tree." For a second, I had a funny picture in my head, but then it was gone.

BEAVER WITH SPECIAL STICKS

"Oh, OK," said Lewis. He took a step forward. I was glad I knew those beaver facts—we had to keep moving. I looked down at his leg. There was blood all over his pants, and somehow we'd lost the T-shirt. How much blood can you lose before you bleed to death? This was something I was starting to think about.

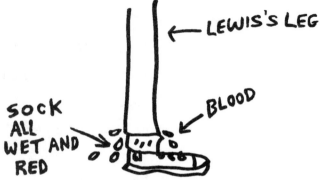

LEWIS'S LEG

BLOOD

SOCK ALL WET AND RED

The Trick

After we'd been walking for about five minutes, Lewis slowed down. He was leaning on me more and more, and I was wishing that Dad's whistle plan had worked. Having Dad help with Lewis would have been a million times better than doing it all by myself. This was almost as scary as a bear, and I didn't like it.

It wasn't easy to keep us moving. The more I pushed forward trying to speed us up, the more Lewis pulled back, slowing us down.

"When your leg's better, I'll go back to the tree with you," I said. "And I'll bring my camera."

I was trying to make Lewis not think about his leg. Mom uses this trick whenever I get hurt. She calls it her distraction technique. The weird thing is, even though I know she's doing it, it still somehow works.

Lewis didn't say anything, but I didn't stop.

"We can go back tomorrow, or the next day."

It was working. I could feel it. We were moving faster again. I kept talking. "We could take food, and eat it up in the tree . . . at the, you know, the spot." I wasn't even thinking about what I was saying. The words were just coming out of my mouth, filling the air. And the words were like horses slowly pulling us out of the woods.

Suddenly Lewis stopped. "Let's do it!" he said.

"What?" I asked. What was he talking about?

"The picnic, and I can bring my underpants—for the photo!"

Lewis pushed my arm away and took a few

steps on his own, with the stick. "I'll probably be better by tomorrow," he said.

He hobbled up the trail ahead of me. We were almost to the road, so I didn't have to worry about making it out of the woods, but now I had a new worry.

"Underpants picnic!" said Lewis. "It will be awesome!"

I followed behind him.

Awesome was not the word I would have used.

Lewis's House

We got to the start of the trail in record time—at least record time for a person with one wrecked leg and one bleeding leg. I was helping Lewis again, but not as much as before.

When we stepped out onto the road, I turned to the right and Lewis turned to the left.

"This way," said Lewis, he pointed left.

I pulled right and shook my head. He was wrong—there weren't any houses to the left. Every single house in Twin Rivers was down the road on the right. I knew that for a fact. I'd lived there my entire life.

"I think you're mixed up," I said. I pointed left. "There aren't any houses over there."

"I don't live in a house," said Lewis. "I live

somewhere better." He looked at me and raised his eyebrows like he wanted me to guess.

I didn't have a clue. There was nothing to the left, only woods and the road.

"Come on, guess!" said Lewis.

I shrugged. "A cave?"

"Wrong!" yelled Lewis. "A super-cool motel! Up there." He pointed left again.

What Lewis was saying and what I knew to be true were two different things that didn't match up. He was right—there was a motel to the left, but it was falling apart and boarded up. No one lived there, no one went there, and everybody said it was full of raccoons and bats. It was definitely not super cool.

"You mean the STAY ON INN?" I asked. "The one with the wood over the windows? The blue one?"

"Yup," said Lewis. "We just bought it. Sage says it's periwinkle. That's a kind of blue." I slowly followed Lewis to the left.

"Who's Sage?"

"My mom," said Lewis. "Wait until you see it. You'll love it! I've always wanted to live in a motel."

We were moving faster now. Lewis didn't need

me talking to keep him going. Suddenly he had lots of energy and lots to say. It probably helped that we were going downhill. I let him talk, but I wasn't really listening. I had my own stuff to think about.

The Motel

As soon as we saw the motel, my brain made an acrostic. I couldn't help it. Sometimes making them helps me feel better about stuff. This time it didn't.

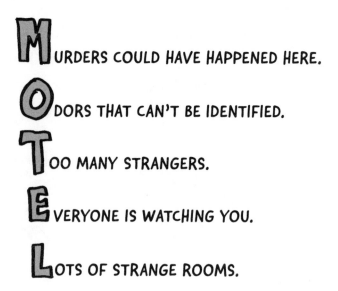

MURDERS COULD HAVE HAPPENED HERE.

ODORS THAT CAN'T BE IDENTIFIED.

TOO MANY STRANGERS.

EVERYONE IS WATCHING YOU.

LOTS OF STRANGE ROOMS.

I looked around for the giant STAY ON INN sign, but it was gone.

"Where's the sign?" I asked.

"Stolen," said Lewis. "Can you believe that? One day it was there, and then the next day it was gone. Stolen in the middle of the night, and we didn't even hear a thing. Sage was pretty mad, but Dave says it's OK, because now we can pick our own name."

"Who's Dave?" I asked.

"My dad," said Lewis. "How come you're asking so many questions about my parents?"

I'd never met anyone who called his parents by their first names before, but I didn't say that. That might sound stupid.

Instead I shrugged my shoulders and said, "Just curious."

The motel wasn't as scary as I was expecting. The wood was off the windows, and the grass was cut. That helped. There was a funny sign over the front door. I was going to ask about it, but I didn't get a chance because suddenly there was a lady standing in the doorway underneath it. I didn't need to ask who it was, because even though Lewis didn't call her Mom, she acted just like one.

Lewis's Family

Lewis's mom didn't notice me until she had Lewis's bleeding leg all fixed up and a bandage on his other leg. I was standing by the door, and they were in the kitchen. When Lewis finally introduced us, she told me to call her Sage.

"Do you go to Barry Hill School?" she asked.

I nodded.

"What grade?"

"Fourth," I answered.

"ME TOO!" yelled Lewis. "We'll be in the same class."

I wasn't excited to be talking about school. In ten days, our break would be over and we'd be back in class. I looked over at Lewis. He was grinning. He didn't seem like it, but maybe he was one of those kids who really liked school.

"You might be in another class," I offered. "I have Mrs. Shipley, and you'd be luckier not to get her." I was about to explain more, but a little kid suddenly burst into the room. He took one look at Lewis and stopped moving.

"What happened? Did you get attacked? Are you going to die?"

"Don't worry. He's fine," said Sage.

"I wasn't worried," said the kid. "Was it a bear?"

"Nope. Underpants!" said Lewis.

"YOU were attacked by underpants?" The kid looked around. Suddenly he noticed me. He pointed.

"*His* underpants?" he asked.

"What the heck?" said Lewis. "Why would Morgan's underpants attack me?" He sat up and cleared his throat. He was getting ready to tell the story, I could tell. Sage could too. She shook her head.

"Another one of Lewis's stories," she said. Suddenly a phone rang in another room. Sage grabbed her first-aid supplies and headed for the door. "I'll have to hear it later," she said. She waved and was gone.

"Who are you?" asked the kid. He was looking at me again. He was younger than us, maybe six or seven years old.

"That's Morgan, my new friend," said Lewis. "And you better be nice to him because he saved my life."

And then Lewis told the story. I was nervous

that he'd break his promise, but he didn't. While I listened, I made up a new acrostic.

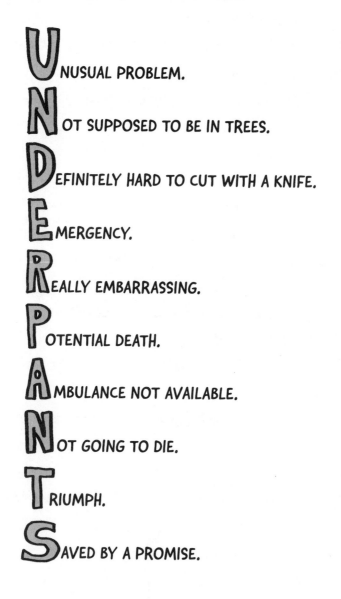

UNUSUAL PROBLEM.

NOT SUPPOSED TO BE IN TREES.

DEFINITELY HARD TO CUT WITH A KNIFE.

EMERGENCY.

REALLY EMBARRASSING.

POTENTIAL DEATH.

AMBULANCE NOT AVAILABLE.

NOT GOING TO DIE.

TRIUMPH.

SAVED BY A PROMISE.

The Way Red

As soon as Lewis finished the story, the kid was full of questions, and mostly they were about the underpants.

"Can I see them? Are you still wearing them?"

"Be patient," said Lewis. "The viewing will be soon." It sounded like he had a plan—a giant underpants plan. I was getting the feeling that Lewis wasn't afraid of anything, not even embarrassment.

The kid looked over at me and smiled. I couldn't tell if it was a wow-you're-a-hero smile or a we-get-to-see-Lewis's-underpants smile. I definitely wasn't with him if it was a smile for the underpants. I smirked back.

"Can we show him the clubhouse?" asked the kid. He was bouncing up and down.

"Good idea," said Lewis. "Lead the way, Red, and we'll follow."

Lewis shifted his weight and grunted as he stood up. It looked like his leg hurt more than he thought it would, but he didn't complain. The kid ran ahead and yelled at us to hurry.

"That's my brother," said Lewis. "His name's Red."

"That's a funny name," I said.

"I know." Lewis smiled. "My parents are creative."

The Most Amazing Clubhouse Ever

Red yelled at us from the back of the motel, probably wondering why we were taking so long. When we finally caught up to him, he was standing on a bunch of wooden boxes next to a large open window. He made sure we were watching, waved, and then dived headfirst through the window.

THE WINDOW

RED

THE BOXES

"What's in there?" I asked. "Won't he get hurt?"

"That's the surprise part," said Lewis. "You go next. I'll go after you." He pushed me forward.

I climbed onto the boxes and peeked in the window. Red was standing on the far side of the room, pointing to the floor. Right below me was the biggest pile of pillows I'd ever seen.

"Flip!" yelled Red.

I jumped, tried to flip, but changed my mind at the last minute and landed on my back. It wasn't what I wanted to do, but it was great! Next time I was definitely going to flip.

I scrambled off the pillows and ran over to Red. When I got there, Lewis was at the window waiting his turn.

"Watch!" he shouted. He jumped and twisted his body into a fast side flip. It was impressive, but maybe not the best choice because the second he landed, he screamed out in pain.

"AAAAAHHHHHHHH!"

I guess flipping with a sore leg wasn't such a good idea. Red and I raced over to help him up.

Once Lewis was standing and back to normal, I got a tour of the clubhouse.

MAP OF THE INSIDE OF THE CLUBHOUSE

OLD CHAIR THAT COVERS UP DOG DOOR

DOG DOOR →

2 MORE CHAIRS

WALL TO WRITE ON

DOOR TO THE HALLWAY IN THE MOTEL BUT BOARDED UP SO YOU CAN'T GO THROUGH IT

WINDOW TO JUMP IN

BOXES OUTSIDE →

PILLOWS AND CUSHIONS TO JUMP ON

STUFF STUCK ON THE WALL WITH DUCT TAPE

SHELVES WITH BOOKS AND SOME TOYS BUT NOT A LOT

"This used to be an office," said Lewis. "But Dave fixed it up for our clubhouse. You come in through the window and leave by this door." Lewis pushed a chair out of the way and showed me what looked like a giant dog door leading back outside.

"It's for dogs, but it works great for us," he said.

It was so big, even a skinny grown-up could have fit through it.

"I wonder what kind of dog that's for," I said. "It's huge."

"I don't care," said Lewis. "I hate dogs."

"Really?" I was surprised. I'd never met a kid who didn't like dogs.

"It's because of the Saint Bernard," said Red. "That's a kind of super-big dog. When Lewis was five, one knocked him down and then stood over him, and wouldn't let him get up for a whole, entire hour."

"It wasn't an hour," said Lewis. "It was ten minutes, but that was long enough. I hate dogs!"

I nodded. Now I understood the hate. I didn't agree with it, but it made sense.

Picnic Planning

The rest of the afternoon went by really fast. We hung out in the clubhouse, messed around with duct tape—Lewis loves duct tape—and drew on the walls with markers. Red and I practiced flips from the window. The only bad thing about the flipping was that you had to go outside and climb the boxes each time you wanted to do it. After that first flip, Lewis didn't do any more flipping. He said he was having a no-flip day until tomorrow.

DOES NOT
FIT VERY
WELL

SURPRISINGLY
STRONG

EXCELLENT
FOR THROWING

DUCT-TAPE
HELMET

DUCT-TAPE
SWORD

DUCT-TAPE
BALLS

I hardly even noticed it was getting dark, until it was almost too late.

"I've got to go." I pointed to the window. "If I don't get home before dark, I'm in big trouble."

Lewis pulled me aside and sent Red outside to get ready for another flip.

"Are we still on for tomorrow?" he whispered. "You know, the underpants picnic." He gestured to the window. "I don't want Red to know, or he'll want to come too."

I tried not to look upset and surprised, but I was both of those things. I thought he'd forgotten about it.

"You need to bring the food," said Lewis. "Sage

makes terrible sandwiches. And bring a camera."
Lewis paused for a second and then added, "Do you
want to meet at the tree at twelve?"

I didn't answer. I was thinking about sandwiches.
How could you make a bad sandwich? Making
sandwiches was easy.

HOW TO MAKE A SANDWICH

I'M DELICIOUS!

1ST PIECE OF BREAD

2ND PIECE OF BREAD

SOME KIND OF FILLING

THE SANDWICH

Lewis thought my not answering meant I didn't
want to meet at the tree, but he was wrong. My
not answering was something entirely different. It
was bigger than the tree. It meant I wanted to
cancel the whole picnic. But his brain was faster

than mine, because before I could say anything, he was talking again.

"OK, we don't have to meet at the tree. We'll meet at your house—that's better. Then I can help you carry the stuff if it's a lot, plus that's more fair." He grinned, nodded, and then without waiting for a yes, no, or anything else, turned to the window and yelled at Red to flip.

There was no time to argue. If I didn't get home before dark, Mom would send Dad out to find me, and there would be nothing good about that.

I didn't want to but I nodded to Lewis. "Fine. I'll see you at my house at twelve." I picked up a marker, scribbled my address on the wall, and scrambled out the dog door. The sky was dark blue. Soon it would be black. I took off running—racing against the stars.

How It Can Be Hard to Make a Sandwich

The next morning when I woke up, the first thing I thought about was the picnic, but for the rest of the morning I did a good job of not thinking about it. At eleven-thirty, I couldn't ignore it anymore. I needed to make the sandwiches. In thirty minutes, Lewis would be knocking on the door, and I couldn't change that.

I decided on peanut butter and jelly, because they're fast, easy, and everyone pretty much likes them. I was halfway done when I noticed the empty jelly jar on the counter. Mom and Dad don't eat jelly, so it had to be Betty. Now I had to find something else to go with the peanut butter that was already on the bread. I dug through the fridge, pulled out a bunch of jars, and lined them up on the counter. There were lots of choices. Blueberry syrup, relish, ranch dressing, lemon curd, mango chutney, applesauce, mint jelly . . . but all of them looked disgusting.

"Hey! Why do you have all this stuff out? What are you doing?" Betty stomped into the kitchen, looked around, and scowled. She was still carrying that ugly brown sweater-thing she'd been knitting for the last two weeks. I pointed to the empty grape jelly jar.

"It's your fault!" I snapped. "You ate it all."

She took a step closer to me. "So what? Mom's going to the store later. Just ask her to get more."

"That'll be too late!" I stammered. I didn't like her standing there, watching me. She was bossy about kitchen stuff, just because she was twelve and allowed to turn on the stove. "I need it now, for sandwiches, for me and Lewis." The arguing wasn't going well.

Betty looked around the kitchen and smiled. "Who's Lewis?" she asked. "Your new invisible friend?"

"No! He's real, and he'll be here in twenty minutes!" I could feel my face turning red—I hated that. Stupid face! I took a step forward and stared at Betty's chin. One day we'd be eye to eye—I couldn't wait.

"He's not like Jason," I teased. "When's he coming over?" Mom says I'm not allowed to make fun of Jason, but this was a special occasion— Betty was asking for it.

"Just you wait," threatened Betty. She pointed her knitting needles at me, turned, and stomped off, probably to find Mom so she could tell on me.

I didn't care. The whole Jason thing was stupid. It was probably number one of all the dumb things I'd ever heard—and I'd heard a lot of dumb things. Jason was Betty's pretend boyfriend. He was 100 percent not real. It was something all her friends were doing. They said it was so they could get practice being girlfriends so that on the day when a real boy asked them out, they'd be ready and would know exactly what to do. Betty had a long wait ahead of her, because for her, that day was going to be NEVER!

A couple of times I'd even caught her pretending to talk to Jason in her room. So embarrassing!

OH, JASON, THANK YOU SO MUCH. YOU SAY THE SWEETEST THINGS.

YOU CAN'T SEE ME, BUT I'M OVER HERE ALMOST THROWING UP! ⟶

HER PILLOW

I looked at the counter. I had all the ingredients for a terrible sandwich. Now I understood what Lewis had been talking about.

Lewis would be here in five minutes. I had to decide fast. I shoved everything back in the fridge and looked in the cupboard. I was lucky—I found some mini marshmallows and chocolate chips. It was an experiment, but maybe it would work. I threw the sandwiches together, wrapped them up, and put them in my backpack. It took only a few minutes to get the other stuff—a bag of tortilla chips, four juice boxes, and my camera. When Lewis rang the doorbell, I wanted to be ready to go.

The Expected Visitor Does Something Unexpected

Lewis was twenty minutes late. For a while I thought he wasn't going to show up, and I wasn't the only one. Betty did too.

Every couple of minutes, she'd walk by and say, "Where's your new friend?" Then she'd make a big show of looking around the room. "Is he here? Where is he? I can't see him."

I tried to ignore her, but it was hard. She was being super annoying, and it was on purpose. Before she started this whole thing, I was just going to take off the second Lewis arrived, but now it was different. Now I wanted Betty to see him. I was going to prove that he was real. That would show her!

When the doorbell finally rang, Betty was in the middle of a sentence. "I can't see—"

RING. RING.

I could tell that she was surprised. *What was she thinking? That I had made-up friends too? And that I'd make lunch for them?*

Lewis was lucky he had a brother—girls were weird.

I let Lewis in and introduced him to Betty. She was polite, but definitely disappointed. I guess she'd been hoping her crazy was contagious. That I had imaginary friends too.

After the introduction, I walked over to the door to leave, but instead of following me, Lewis walked toward Betty. Maybe he could sense her strangeness. Lewis seemed to like strange things.

BETTY AS A VACUUM, SUCKING LEWIS TOWARD HER

"What are you knitting?" asked Lewis. Now both Betty and I were surprised.

"Uh . . . a sweater," said Betty.

"Wow, that's hard to make," said Lewis. He shook his head. "I made a scarf once, and a really bad hat, but I couldn't make a sweater." He pointed at Betty's brown mess. "That's cool."

"It's the back of the sweater," said Betty. She held it out for Lewis to admire.

"Looks good," said Lewis. "Nice stitches." Then he turned back to me and said, "Let's go."

I nodded. My mouth didn't have words—I was stunned. Lewis followed me back to the door.

He turned one more time, said "Bye, Betty," and then slammed the door behind us.

The Kind of Questions That Can't Wait

It took me a minute or two to get my brain working, but when I did, it was filled with questions.

"WHAT WAS THAT? Were you serious? You know about knitting? Do you knit?"

Lewis didn't seem surprised, or embarrassed, or any of the other things I would have expected. He just answered my questions like nothing was strange.

"I don't knit now, but I used to. I'm not very good at it. I learned to knit at my old school. We all had to do it. I really wanted to make a sweater, but it took me forever to just make a scarf. Do you knit?"

"No!" I spluttered and held in my laughter. If I started knitting, Betty's head would probably explode.

SECOND ONE   SECOND TWO

"It's kind of fun," said Lewis. "But not easy. You should try it."

I nodded. But it was a lie. I wasn't going to knit. Ever! I was sure about that.

"Oh, hey, I remembered the underpants," said Lewis. "In case you were worried." He pointed to a lump in his coat pocket.

I shook my head. "I wasn't worried," I said. "And I'm not touching them."

"They're clean," said Lewis.

"It doesn't matter!" I stopped walking. We were at the start of the trail.

"OK. OK," said Lewis. "I was mostly only joking."

Lewis walked ahead of me. He'd made a fast recovery and was hardly limping.

"Stupid underpants," I mumbled. And then I jogged to catch up.

A boy who knits, and an underpants picnic! Could this day get any weirder? I shook my head. *No, definitely not.*

The Tree

It was easy to find the tree. Lewis was worried about beavers again, but when we got there, every single stick was exactly where I'd left it.

"Here—take my photo before we go up," said Lewis. He pulled the underpants out of his pocket, and spun them around on his hand.

I moved back to take the photo and get out of the line of fire. I didn't trust him. What Lewis thought was funny and what I thought was funny were probably not the same thing, and I didn't want to take any chances.

A second after I took the picture, Lewis was gone. I'd never seen him climb before. He was like a squirrel, even with his sore legs.

"Come on! Let's get started," yelled Lewis.

I waved and did my best, but he was already at our tree meeting spot before I was even six feet off the ground.

"What did you bring?" asked Lewis. He grabbed the backpack while I wedged myself in between two branches. This was a lot higher than I'd remembered. I looked down. I could see the ground below us, but it wasn't close.

"You're lucky you didn't kill yourself," I said.

Lewis rubbed his leg. "Only this one still hurts, but it's not bad," he said. But I caught him wincing a second later. Somehow that made me feel better. It's hard to be friends with a superhero.

A. LEWIS HAS SUPER-SPEEDY LEGS.

B. LEWIS IS AN AMAZING JUMPER.

The First-Ever Underpants Picnic

Lewis pulled the tortilla chips out of the backpack, put them on his lap, and then dug around to see what else he could find.

"Hey, be careful," I said, but it was too late—the chips and a juice box were on their way down to the ground.

"Oops," said Lewis. "Oh well, we can have those for dessert." He pulled out another juice box and stuck it under his arm. "You brought sandwiches, right?"

I was about to tell him about Betty eating all the grape jelly, but before I could, he had unwrapped a sandwich and was sniffing it.

"Peanut butter," I said.

"Oh good," said Lewis. "I thought it might be flax butter."

I made a face. I didn't know what that was, but it sounded gross.

"I told you," said Lewis. "Sage makes bad sandwiches."

He dug around in the backpack, found the other sandwich, and tossed it over to me. I was lucky to catch it. I scowled. Didn't he learn anything? Half our lunch was already on the ground.

"Good catch," said Lewis. He gave me a thumbs-up and grinned.

I unwrapped the sandwich.

"Wait! Don't eat!" he shouted. "We've got to do this first." He fished in his pocket and pulled out the underpants. Then very carefully, he hung them on the stick that had given him the wedgie. I guess that was more important than lunch.

"The wedgie spot," said Lewis. "Take a picture." He leaned in close and smiled. I snapped the shot. I didn't want my picture with the underpants, so Lewis took one of me just sitting in the tree.

LEWIS IN THE TREE

ME IN THE TREE

Sandwich Inventions

Lewis said the sandwich was the best peanut butter sandwich he'd ever eaten. Even though that was a nice compliment, I took the extra juice box. He could have the one on the ground. That seemed fair.

YOU BET I'M DELICIOUS! I'M FILLED WITH MARSHMALLOWS AND CHOCOLATE CHIPS!

We'd finished lunch and were just about to head down when I noticed something on the ground. It caught my eye—it was bigger than a squirrel. I motioned for Lewis to be quiet and look down. My first thought was a bear, but it wasn't furry. It was slimy-looking and shiny. *What kind of animals are slimy?* I looked over at Lewis, but he didn't look back. He kept staring below. I looked down again.

The creature was bent over, doing something on the ground. Sniffing? Looking for food? Suddenly, it stood up. It was enormous, bigger than I was expecting. Its huge head turned back and forth, looking up and down the trail, and then very slowly it looked up. I froze. Seconds later its dark alien eyes stared straight at me. I couldn't breathe. I couldn't swallow. I knew what was next. I was going to die.

EYES LOOKING RIGHT AT ME

I wanted to look at Lewis but I couldn't. My body was frozen. The creature paced around to the other side of the tree and looked up again. I knew what it was doing. It was looking for a way up. It was going to come up to get us. I forced my eyes to look at Lewis. His face was white. This did not give me courage.

When I looked down again, the creature had

moved away from the tree and onto the path. It was still, and then suddenly its head spun around twice—360 degrees times two! How could it do that? I looked at Lewis. Did he just see that? His eyes widened. When I looked back, the creature was gone. I caught another glimpse of it through the trees. It was running down the path, headed for the road. I should have felt relieved, but I didn't.

I felt like I was going to throw up.

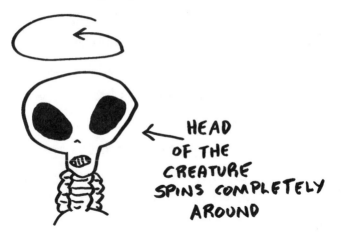

HEAD OF THE CREATURE SPINS COMPLETELY AROUND

THIS IS NOT NATURAL!

What It Was

Lewis and I were quiet for what seemed like an hour. We didn't move, we didn't speak, and we hardly breathed. At least I didn't. Finally I felt safe enough to whisper, "Did you see that?" It was a stupid question. Of course he'd seen it.

"What was it?" asked Lewis.

"Alien!" I whispered. "I know about them. My dad has some books. That was an alien!"

"We've got to tell someone," said Lewis. "And we've got to get out of here. What if it comes back?"

I hadn't thought about that. Maybe it had gone to get help. Maybe a whole bunch of aliens were on their way back right now. Lewis was right—we needed to leave. Two seconds later, we were climbing out of the tree as fast as we could. Lewis was behind me. Three feet from the bottom, I let go and jumped. It was a clumsy landing. I did not land on my feet. When I got up, my pants were soaking wet.

"Alien slime!" said Lewis. He pointed and backed away.

I looked at my pants, and then the ground. Lewis's juice box was squashed flat, right where I'd fallen. It wasn't slime. I pointed. Lewis took a step closer.

"That's OK," he whispered. "I wasn't thirsty."

I brushed off my pants, but it didn't make a difference. It still looked like pee.

JUICE BOX SQUASHED FLAT

Lewis wasn't paying attention to me. He was walking around the tree, searching the ground.

"What are you looking for?" I asked. We didn't have time for this. We needed to go. Any second now, a horde of aliens could show up. It made me shiver.

"The chips," said Lewis. "I can't find them. It took them."

"Who cares?" I said. "Let's go." My backpack was on and I was ready to run.

"OK," said Lewis. He gave the tree a final look and then sprinted down the path ahead of me. Even though the path to the left was shorter, we went right—opposite from the alien.

All I wanted to do was get home. I ran fast, faster than I'd ever run before—I even passed Lewis. If I hadn't been so scared, I would have been impressed with myself.

1ST
FOR MORGAN FOR
RUNNING SUPER
FAST IN AN ALIEN
CRISIS

Home

As soon as we got to my house, we ran inside and locked the door. After a few minutes of hard breathing, I started to feel normal. Now I was more excited than scared. I couldn't believe what had just happened, and neither could Mom and Dad. They made us swear three or four times that what we were saying was the truth and not some kind of made-up story.

Dad said, "I don't want to call someone about this and then have it blow up in my face because you boys saw a possum and thought it was an alien."

Lewis shook his head. "It definitely wasn't a possum!"

I nodded in agreement and held out my arms to show how big it was. Mom didn't say anything. She just looked worried. I caught her looking at my pants. I was about to say it was apple juice, but Dad grabbed me by the shoulder and pointed to some paper on a table. "Draw it! Each of you. I want to know what we're dealing with."

Even though our drawings were different, Dad seemed satisfied.

"It had three legs. You missed one," said Lewis. He was looking at my drawing.

"No, it had two," I said. I pointed at his paper. "And you made the head too small. Don't you remember? It was huge."

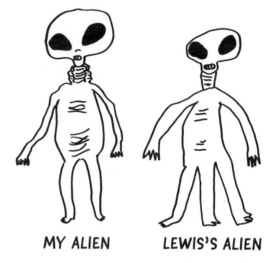

MY ALIEN   LEWIS'S ALIEN

Lewis looked down and nodded. "Oh yeah. Can I do it again, Mr. Henry? Can I fix it?"

"No time!" said Dad. "If this thing is still around, we need to tell someone about it right now. Let's go."

Dad grabbed our pictures and hustled us into the car. It was a short ride to the police station, but it felt like forever.

"It's too bad you didn't use your camera," said

Lewis. He was right. Our drawings were pretty bad. A photo would have been much better. Plus then Lewis would have seen that I was right—the alien had two legs.

What Happened at the Police Station?

When we got to the station, Dad went up to one of the police officers and said, "Gary, I've got something you might want to have a look at." Dad motioned for Lewis and me to sit down on a bench that was against the wall, and then he and Gary walked to the other side of the room. I'd never been in the police station before. It was kind of disappointing. I thought it would be high-tech, but mostly it just looked like a big office, kind of like the post office, only not as busy.

Lewis nudged me. "Look! He's telling him about it," he said.

I looked over. Dad was holding out our drawings and pointing to them. He was excited. If there was one thing Dad loved, it was anything to do with aliens.

When he was ten, he saw strange lights in the sky, and ever since, he's been alien crazy. That's probably why he didn't think we were lying about the alien—we didn't have to convince him. He was already a believer.

"I bet they'll be tearing out of here any second now," said Lewis. He pulled his legs in from the aisle so the policemen would be able to get by. We waited, and waited, but nothing happened.

"Maybe they need special uniforms or something," said Lewis. I hadn't thought about that. Getting ready probably took a while. Thinking about what we were going to see next made the waiting more exciting.

SPECIAL ALIEN-CATCHING UNIFORM

MASK WITH AIR IN CASE ALIEN SHOOTS POISONOUS STUFF

HELMET WITH ALIEN SENSOR ON TOP

SEE-IN-THE-DARK GLASSES

PROTECTIVE VEST

AIR TANK

FLAME THROWER

HANDY EXTRA SUPPLIES

SPECIAL BOOTS

Finally, after what seemed like forever, Dad came over. He was smiling.

"They're going to look into it," he said. His smile wasn't real. I could tell. I glanced around the station. Nothing was different than when we'd arrived. There was no rushing, no frenzy, no panic, no action . . . no nothing!

"I know you wanted a SWAT team," said Dad, "but I don't think that's going to happen. They're sending a police officer out to walk the trail."

Dad was going to say more, but suddenly Officer Gary was standing next to him. He looked bigger close up. Maybe it was the gun. It was hard not to stare at it.

Officer Gary looked down at us and said, "So you boys saw something in the woods." Lewis and I both nodded.

"Are you sure it wasn't a coyote? We've had a couple of those around here recently."

"No, sir," said Lewis. "It was an alien."

Officer Gary squinted and stared straight at me. I felt uncomfortable, and even though I wasn't lying, I could feel my face getting red and my ears starting to burn. I didn't say anything.

Officer Gary cleared his throat, looked at our drawings one more time, and then handed them back to us.

"I know where to find you if I have any questions," he said. He smiled as he watched us get up, but there was nothing about him that was one bit friendly.

GIANT MAN WITH A GUN.

ANGRY-LOOKING ON THE OUTSIDE.

REALLY SCARY.

YOUR FRIENDLY LOCAL POLICE OFFICER?

How to Make Yourself Feel Better

As soon as we got out of the police station, Dad said, "Let's get some ice cream."

I had the feeling I wasn't the only one disappointed by the no-SWAT-team thing.

The ice cream place is next door, so we were there in about ten seconds. I always get chocolate, but it's fun to look at the other flavors, just in case I change my mind. Lewis was having a hard time choosing. He wanted to taste absolutely everything.

"Can I try banana fudge, bubble blast, and strawberry swirl?" he asked. "Oh, and chocolate brownie too?" I had a feeling we were going to be standing there for a while.

"Well, at least they didn't laugh in our faces," said Dad. He was talking about the police station and Officer Gary.

"I don't think Officer Gary laughs at anything," said Lewis.

Dad nodded. Lewis was probably right about that.

"I wish I'd been there with you boys," said Dad. "I wish I'd seen what you saw."

"I wish we'd used the camera," said Lewis. He was right—a photo would have changed everything. It was exactly what we needed. It would have been proof!

PHOTO IS PROOF

Lewis looked down and crumpled up the drawing in his hand. Just then, a man next to him tapped him on the shoulder.

"Do you mind if I see that?" he asked. He pointed to Lewis's drawing.

"Can I help you?" asked Dad. He stepped in front of Lewis.

"I write for the *Twin Rivers Times*," said the man. "Can I buy you all some ice cream, and have a little chat?"

"Sure," said Dad. He was smiling again, but this time his smile was real. "You're just the guy we need." Then he put a hand on my shoulder and said, "You can order something big. I'm not paying."

NORMAL-SIZE
ICE CREAM

SUPER-SIZE
ICE CREAM

Twin Rivers Times

It was exciting to talk to a real reporter. Lewis and I told him the whole story about three or four times, and in between he had lots of questions. I was glad that Lewis didn't mention the underpants.

Dad was happy to be talking to the reporter. It meant he'd get free publicity for his store in the paper. Dad's store is Rudy's Sporting Goods, and he's always looking for a way to bring in more customers. It's easy to see how his brain works. By the end of the conversation, Dad had already decided to have a huge special Alien Sale when the article came out.

"It'll be savings out of this world," said Dad.

Lewis smiled and held up his hand like a high five, but I just groaned. It's not easy having a dorky dad.

I was hoping we'd get our photos in the paper,

but the reporter said he was going to use our drawings instead. It kind of made me wish I'd spent more time on it, but Dad said not to worry—it looked fine.

"When's this coming out?" asked Dad.

"Tomorrow," said the reporter. "First thing."

Dad rubbed his hands together. "I can't wait. Now we'll get some action." He leaned over and put his arms around me and Lewis. "Someone's going to catch this creature. It's going to be huge!"

That surprised me. I hadn't thought about that. Could they catch it alive? How? What if it had laser eyes or something? Dad was right—this was big.

"One more thing," said Lewis. "I don't know if this is important, but it likes tortilla chips. It stole our whole bag of them."

I nodded in agreement. I'd forgotten about that.

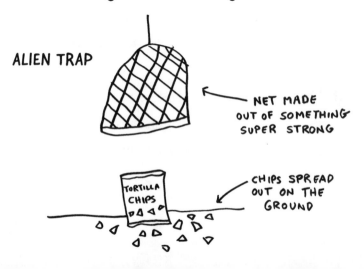

ALIEN TRAP

NET MADE OUT OF SOMETHING SUPER STRONG

TORTILLA CHIPS

CHIPS SPREAD OUT ON THE GROUND

After the reporter left, we drove Lewis home. Dad was filled with energy and talked the whole way. Right before we got to the motel, he stopped the car and turned around in his seat.

"I'm really proud of you boys," he said. "It's not easy to step up and tell the truth in a situation like this. I just want you to know I believe in you."

I was surprised. I didn't know what to say. Lewis spoke first.

"Thank you, Mr. Henry." This time he gave Dad a real high five.

"Alien high five," said Dad. He moved his hand over toward me. It was corny, but I did it.

What Was Surprisingly Easy?

I thought it would be hard to get Lewis's parents, Dave and Sage, to believe us about the alien, but it wasn't. At first they were mostly surprised. Then Dad's energy got to them and made them worked up about it too. For some reason, no one was worried about an alien attack. Maybe that's because the sky looked normal. If giant alien

spaceships had been flying all over, things would
have been a lot different.

ALIEN SHIPS

AHHH! ALIENS!!!

Lewis was excited to tell them about the tortilla
chips.

"I didn't see it carrying the chips," said Lewis.
"But when we got out of the tree, the chips were
gone. So it took them. Maybe it put them in a secret
pouch or something."

Dave nodded. "Well,"
he said, "I suppose
anything is possible."

THIS IS WHERE
I KEEP MY
SNACKS.

The Bad Thing

Dad and Lewis's parents decided that it wasn't safe for Lewis and me to wander around town anymore, at least until there was more information about the alien.

"It's for your protection," said Dad. "Once this story comes out, every nutcase alien chaser in the country is going to be up here trying to track it. And I don't want them chasing you down for special hints."

Lewis's parents nodded in agreement.

Dad pointed to the motel. "Are you open for business? I bet you could be busy very soon."

I couldn't tell if Lewis's parents liked that idea or not. Lewis's mom just nodded and looked tired. After that, Dad and I got into the car to leave.

"You can drop Lewis off at our place in the morning, if you like," said Dad. "I'll be around all day, and I'm sure the boys will have lots to talk about. Maybe we can even get them to read the paper."

He said this last part to be funny, but he was right—tomorrow I was definitely going to read the paper. I could already imagine it. I smiled and waved to Lewis.

Tomorrow Is Today

I thought I would wake up extra early, but that didn't happen. Instead, I slept late, even later than normal.

Mom was downstairs with Betty when I walked into the kitchen. Betty was complaining about something, but I couldn't tell what. Maybe she and Jason had had a good-morning mix-up. I thought of what it could be and smiled, but didn't say anything.

JASON

"Look! You're famous," said Betty. She pointed to the newspaper on the table. "Of course our town is so small they'll write about anything."

I ignored her snarky comment and ran over to the open paper. Sure enough, there was our story, right on the bottom of page three. I liked the title—"Extraterrestrial Enjoys Tortillas." The article wasn't as long as I thought it would be, but still, it was good! Our names and drawings were in the article too. Right under our drawings, it said, "*Drawings of the aliens spotted by the boys.*" Dad must have been happy too because it mentioned that I was the son of a store owner in town. Dad loves to see his store's name in print.

I pointed to the paper. "Hey, Mom. They made a mistake. It says 'aliens,' but it should say 'alien,' because we saw only one."

Mom shook her head. "It doesn't surprise me," she said. "That paper is always getting things wrong."

"I don't believe it," said Betty.

"I know," I said. "I don't either. How could a newspaper make a mistake like that?"

"No, not that," said Betty. "That you saw it!"

I couldn't believe what I was hearing. "WHAT? You think we lied?"

"Not on purpose," said Betty. "More like you were confused or something. Why were you up in that tree anyway?"

"We just were," I said. I felt my face getting red.

"And an alien from outer space decided that he would just come down and bounce around under your tree." Betty looked at Mom. "I don't know. It sounds made up, don't you think?"

"It didn't bounce!" I said. Now I was mad.

Mom walked over between the two of us and held out her arms. "That's enough from both of you." She sighed. "I'm sure we'll have some answers soon. The police are investigating."

Betty left the kitchen, but that didn't help—she'd already ruined everything. Now I was nervous. I couldn't eat, not even the banana muffins Mom had made, and they were my favorites. It wasn't fair. While I waited for Lewis, I made up a new acrostic. It was Betty's fault.

AT FIRST IT'S EXCITING TO SEE AN ALIEN.

LATER ON IT'S NOT.

IT'S HARD TO SEE SOMETHING NO ONE ELSE DID.

EVERYONE THINKS YOU MADE IT UP.

NOBODY WILL BELIEVE YOU.

Lewis didn't come over until almost lunchtime. I could tell that he'd seen the paper because he was carrying about twenty copies of it.

"We're famous!" he shouted. "Wouldn't it be cool if someone caught the alien, and we got to be on TV with it?"

ALIEN IN SEE-THROUGH BOX THAT IT CAN'T GET OUT OF

VERY, VERY STRONG BOX

Lewis was right—that would be cool. But Betty had put a new thought in my head, and that thought was making it hard to be as happy about everything as he was. What if everyone thought we were lying? I almost told Lewis about it, but he was suddenly halfway across the room. He had spotted the muffins. He grabbed one in each hand

and held them up. It was a good idea—I was hungry now too.

"I like how your mom doesn't put vegetables and seeds in muffins," he said. "These look a lot better than the ones Sage makes." He took a bite. "Yup, they're good."

I made a mental note—*Do not eat muffins at Lewis's house.*

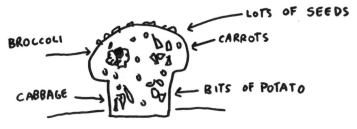

Betty

"Who drew that?" Lewis pointed to a card on the fridge. It had the words YOU'RE AMAZING on top, and underneath was a picture of a boy standing next to a horse.

"Betty," I answered. I wanted to say more, but I didn't.

"Wow," said Lewis. "She's really good at art. What's the amazing part? Did the horse do something?"

I didn't answer. I'd promised Mom that I wouldn't tell anyone about Jason, but Lewis wasn't anyone. It was only my third day of knowing him, and I'd already saved his life, seen an alien, and been in the paper with him. That had to mean something. I made sure Betty wasn't around, and then in a whisper, I told him about Jason.

"So she drew him a card, and he's not even real?" asked Lewis.

I could tell that he couldn't believe it. I nodded. It felt good to have someone else in the Betty-Is-Crazy Club.

What I Thought Lewis Would Say

Lewis tapped the card. "Wow, she must really like art to go to all that trouble for nothing," said Lewis. It wasn't the response I was expecting, but that was Lewis. He was hard to predict.

About five minutes later, Betty walked into the kitchen. She was still dragging around her knitting. From across the room, it looked like Chewbacca's fur—brown, messy, and strange. She was lucky that Jason was imaginary because no real boy-friend was ever going to wear that thing. But I didn't say anything, because that would have been stupid—Betty's good at headlocks.

THE BETTY HEADLOCK
IN ACTION

Betty looked at the plate of muffins. They were almost gone. She was probably going to be mad.

"Do you want some apple juice?" she asked. She was facing Lewis.

"Sure," said Lewis. He took another muffin.

"Me too," I said, but I had a feeling she wouldn't get me any. Betty put her knitting on the table next to Lewis and went to the fridge.

"Hey, you did more on your sweater," said Lewis. He poked it with his finger. "Are you almost done?"

It didn't sound like a compliment, but Betty answered like it was.

"Yes, thank you," she said.

When she came back to the table, she was smiling, and had three glasses of juice—one for each of us. I didn't say anything, but my brain thought of a new acrostic.

LOOKS REGULAR, BUT HE ISN'T.

EVERYTHING HE DOES WILL SURPRISE YOU.

WILL SAY WHAT YOU DON'T EXPECT.

IS FRIENDLY TO EVERYONE.

STRANGE THINGS HAPPEN AROUND HIM.

Later That Afternoon

After all the muffins were gone, Lewis and I went up to my room. There's something about having a new friend in your room for the first time that feels kind of uncomfortable. It's like excited and nervous mixed together. You want to show him your stuff, but at the same time you don't want him to see something embarrassing and then think you're lame. Just to be safe, I pushed Binky under my pillow. Lewis didn't need to see my stuffed monkey.

THINGS THAT COULD INSTANTLY MAKE YOU FEEL LAME

YOUR
BLANKIE

TEDDY BEAR
MOBILE

BABY TOY

LOVE NOTES
FROM YOUR MOM

Mostly I was excited to show Lewis my books and magazines about aliens. They used to be Dad's, so they're old, but they're still great.

"Let's look for a picture of our alien," I said. "Maybe there'll be information about it." I was happy when Lewis agreed.

Even though Betty had been nice in the kitchen, her old words about me and Lewis seeing the alien were still floating in my brain. It would be nice to have proof, even if it was someone else's proof.

Looking through everything took a lot longer than I thought it would, but finally we were finished. Lewis tossed the last book onto my bed.

"Nothing," he said. "Maybe these are too old."

I thought about it, and nodded. There were probably advances in alien research that we didn't know about.

"We could go to the library," I said.

Lewis scrunched up his nose. "It's hard to be quiet in there," he said. "I have a very loud voice."

I shook my head. "Well, you'll just have to whisper, plus it's important. We have to do research." And then because I could tell that he didn't believe me, I told him about what Betty had said, and how sometimes it can be complicated to see something different.

LOOK OVER THERE. IT'S THOSE BOYS WHO THINK THEY SAW AN ALIEN.

The Library

Lewis and I had our coats on and were just heading out the door when Mom suddenly appeared out of nowhere.

"Where do you think you're going?" she asked.

I was happy I didn't need to lie—plus I was about to get extra points for going to the library on a nonschool day. I couldn't wait to answer her.

"We're going to the library, to do research on aliens," I said. I watched closely and waited for her to be filled with surprise.

Mom shook her head. "I don't think so. It's too dangerous!" She crossed her arms. "I want you here, in the house. Where I know where you are. The library isn't safe!"

Instead of her being surprised, now it was me! I couldn't believe what she was saying. The library was dangerous? How? Was the alien going to be there looking at books?

"MOM! The library doesn't have aliens!"

I looked at Lewis. He shrugged. He didn't really want to go anyway.

I'M AN ALIEN! I WONDERED WHAT I WAS.

ALIEN AT THE LIBRARY

"Don't be ridiculous!" Mom scrunched up her face. "Of course the alien isn't at the library. It's other people I'm worried about—strangers. This isn't like the time with Mrs. Lee and the bear. A lot of people are going to be interested in what you saw. It's different."

"Is it a bigger news story than the bear?" I asked.

"I don't know." Mom shook her head. She was getting frustrated. "Probably, if they find something."

I turned to Lewis. "You weren't here when the bear thing happened, but it was huge! And Mrs. Lee got to be on TV. So if this is bigger than the bear, we'll definitely be on TV." Lewis and I did a high five.

"Oh, no you won't. No TV! The newspaper is bad enough. The phone hasn't stopped ringing all morning. I can't get a thing done. Not even the laundry." Mom put her hands on her hips and stared down at us. It was her serious face, the one that means *Don't talk back! We are done discussing this.* I was guessing that Lewis's mom had the same face, because he knew exactly what to do too. We both just stood there, nodded, and didn't say a word.

WHAT I WOULD SAY TO MOM IF I WASN'T BLOCKED FROM TALKING BY HER SERIOUS FACE

Being Stuck

There's a big difference between being stuck in the house and just staying in the house because you want to. Lewis and I tried to find fun things to do, but nothing worked. All we could think about was how we were like prisoners and not allowed to leave. The only interesting thing we did all day was spy on Betty while she was pretend-talking to Jason. It was hard not to crack up, but I kept reminding myself of her headlock powers, and that pretty much did the trick.

When Lewis left to go home, I went upstairs and drew a better picture of the alien. Mom said we weren't going to be on TV, but she could be wrong. And if she was, I didn't want to be embarrassed by a crummy drawing. A lot more people would see it on TV than in the newspaper.

After dinner we all watched the news, but they didn't mention the alien. I think Dad was even more disappointed than I was. I didn't say anything, but I had a feeling that our big alien story wasn't going to be so big after all.

Stuck Times Two

Mom must have talked to Lewis's mom, because the next morning when she dropped me off, Lewis said, "We have to stay around here. Sage says so." I was OK with that—Lewis's house was a lot more fun than my house.

"Let's go to the back. Red and I have an invention."

I followed Lewis past the clubhouse to the back of the motel. Lewis pointed to the roof of a small shed. Red was standing on it. "Go!" shouted Lewis.

Red jumped, flipped, and landed on a stack of mattresses, and then without stopping, continued rolling until he had come to the end of a long mattress pathway. I'd never seen anything like it! I ran closer for a better view.

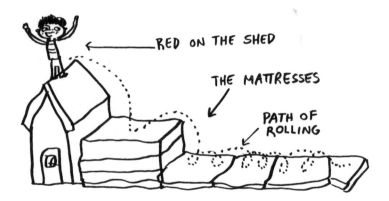

RED ON THE SHED

THE MATTRESSES

PATH OF ROLLING

"Where'd you get all these?" I pointed to the mattresses. Just when I thought Lewis had the coolest house ever, it got cooler.

Lewis ran to the mattresses and did a flip. "Dave got new mattresses for all the guest rooms, so he gave us these old ones."

"And people are going to stay in the rooms

starting tomorrow," said Red. "And two of them are real alien hunters."

Lewis scowled and jabbed Red in the arm.

"I told you to save that part! Now you ruined the surprise."

Red rubbed his arm, but I could tell it was more show than pain.

Sometimes I did the same thing when Betty picked on me. At first she used to feel bad that she'd hurt me, but now she was used to me faking and didn't care anymore. Lewis was the same. He didn't even pay attention to Red.

BETTY
TALKING TO
ME

LEWIS
TALKING TO
RED

"Real alien hunters? Are you sure?" I studied Lewis to see if he was joking, but he nodded, and Red, who was standing next to him, nodded about a hundred times.

"This is it!" I said. "Now we're definitely going to be famous."

Once they caught the alien, everything would change. Betty was wrong. We'd be heroes! I had a ton of questions.

"What kind of cage do you think they're going to use? Maybe they don't use a cage. Maybe they use a net. Do you think they'll kill it?"

"I hope not," said Lewis. "I bet they catch it and keep it alive."

"I don't care what Mom says," I said. "If they catch that alien, I'm going on TV!"

"Me too!" said Lewis. "And I'm glad you said that, because Dave said I could be on TV no problem, and it'll be way more fun if you're there too."

I should have been happy, but instead I frowned. Now, not only did Lewis have a cooler house, he also had cooler parents. The only thing I had better than him was muffins.

DON'T BE SAD.
DELICIOUS MUFFINS
ARE IMPORTANT.

Lewis, Red, and I spent the whole rest of the day moving the mattresses around and coming up with new challenges. It was a lot more fun than watching Betty knit.

Late in the afternoon, we went up to Lewis's room. It was the first time I was seeing his room, and he wanted to show me the scarf he had made.

ISN'T IT COOL?

YEAH, I GUESS.

REALLY
THINKING IT'S
NOT VERY COOL

Lewis's room was fine, except for one thing, and it was Lewis's favorite new thing, and it was hanging right above his bed. And Lewis wasn't one bit embarrassed.

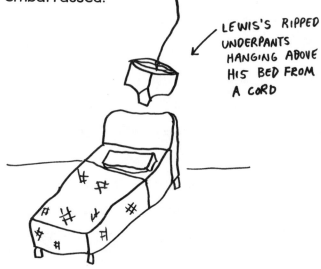

LEWIS'S RIPPED UNDERPANTS HANGING ABOVE HIS BED FROM A CORD

Alien Hunters

The next morning before Mom could stop me, I had Dad drive me over to Lewis's house. I didn't say anything about the alien hunters. Dad would have been excited about them, but he would have also told Mom. And if Mom knew I was talking to strangers, she'd have me back home, stuck in the house, in no time. Instead I told Dad about the mattresses.

"I was wondering why you wanted to get over there so fast," he said. "I wouldn't tell your mom about the flipping though. You know how she worries." I nodded. I could already imagine what Mom would make me wear if she knew I was jumping off a shed.

OUTFIT THAT IS NO FUN!

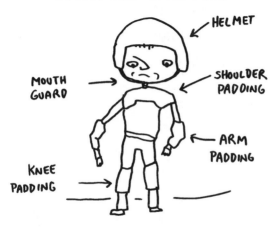

HELMET

MOUTH GUARD

SHOOLDER PADDING

ARM PADDING

KNEE PADDING

As soon as we got to Lewis's house, I jumped out of the car and ran to the front door.

"Have fun!" shouted Dad. I waved back. Maybe he wasn't so uncool after all. At least he didn't say be careful.

I knocked and waited for someone to let me in. When Lewis opened the door, I asked about the hunters.

"Are they here yet?"

Lewis shook his head. "Not yet, but when they get here, I'm definitely going to tell them about the tortilla chips." He nodded to himself. "That's going to help catch it."

"Do you think they'll want to go to the tree?" I asked.

Lewis nodded. "Definitely! To find clues and stuff. It's a good thing you put those sticks around it. It's almost like we were ready for it to happen."

I sighed. It was good Betty wasn't around because I knew exactly what she would have said.

I was disappointed when Dad showed up at five-thirty. He was a whole half hour early, and Lewis and I were still waiting for the alien hunters. Now I was going to miss them.

"Bummer," said Lewis. He understood! The unloading of all the cool supplies was the best part. Plus I wanted to be there to help Lewis tell the story.

I begged Dad to let me stay longer, but he said no, Mom had dinner on the table, and she'd made it special for me.

"You'll get over it," Dad said. "You can come back and jump on those mattresses tomorrow." For a second I was tempted to tell him about the alien hunters, but I didn't. If I did, there'd be no tomorrow.

I waved to Lewis and followed Dad to the car. It helped only a little that we were having lasagna.

New Things

When I got home, the smell of dinner changed my mood. Two minutes ago, I wasn't hungry, but now I was starving. Mom and Betty were already sitting at the table waiting for us.

"There's a letter for you on the counter," said Mom. "It came a few days ago, but in all the excitement I forgot about it. You can look at it after dinner."

Normally I'd want to rip the letter open right away, but my brain was thinking about other things. It's pretty hard to think about regular stuff when you're thinking about aliens.

WHAT THE ALIEN HUNTERS WERE GOING TO BE LIKE

Betty was happy about something too. She was in a great mood.

"Guess what," she said.

"I give up," said Dad. He hates guessing games.

"I almost finished my sweater. All I have to do is put it together."

"That's great," said Dad, but I could tell he didn't really care. Why would he? The sweater was ugly, and on top of that, it was for someone who didn't even exist. I wondered if he was worried that Betty might give it to him for his birthday in two weeks. If she did, then he'd have to wear it to prove how much he liked it and loved Betty. Poor Dad. I looked up. He was scratching his neck, probably thinking about it being itchy. It looked itchy. Really itchy! Like maybe the itchiest sweater ever made.

WHAT BETTY'S SWEATER COULD BE USED FOR

The Letter

After dinner, I went to my room. Mom was helping Betty put her sweater together on the kitchen table, and I didn't want to be near it. It looked like a dead thing.

I pulled out some of Dad's alien books and started going through them. When I talked to the alien hunters, I wanted to impress them. I needed some big words. I was just memorizing *interstellar* when Betty burst into the room.

"You forgot your letter," she said. She threw it onto the bed. "Maybe it's a love letter?" she teased. "Or maybe it's from the alien—an alien love letter!"

Part of me wanted to be mad at her for teasing me, but the picture in my brain made me laugh instead.

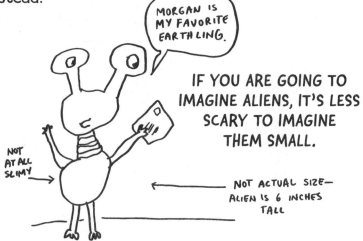

"A letter from an alien would be cool," I said.

"Yeah, you're right," said Betty. "But don't get your hopes up. It's probably just a birthday invitation."

I picked up the letter and shook it. There was something heavy inside.

"BETTY!" It was Mom calling from downstairs.

"I'm coming!" yelled Betty, and she ran out of the room.

I shook the letter a couple more times, and then gave up guessing and ripped it open. A key dropped out onto the floor. I pulled a folded piece of paper out of the envelope and read it. After reading it three more times, I was still confused. There were only two possibilities: either Lewis and I were in big trouble or we were in the middle of some kind of mystery.

Dear Morgan and Lewis,
Please use the enclosed key to open my side garage door. Please come at 2 p.m. on Friday. Do not let anyone follow you. I have answers about the alien.

Your friend,
Mr. Lee

Falling asleep is not easy when you have a mystery in your brain and a key in your hand.

The Next Morning

The first thing I did when I woke up was to make a note for Mom and Dad. I'd seen people do stuff like that on TV. If there was trouble, I wanted Mom and Dad to know where I was. Mr. Lee wasn't dangerous—our whole family knew him—but still it was better to be careful. Plus the whole key thing was kind of mysterious.

It was like when you hear spooky music in a movie—it made me feel uneasy.

Dear Mom and Dad,

If I am missing, go to Mr. Lee's garage to find me. I'll be there at 2 p.m. on Friday. It has something to do with the alien. Don't worry. But if it's past 5 p.m., then maybe you should worry. And if you call the police, don't call Officer Gary.

Love,

Morgan

I put my note under my pillow and shoved Mr. Lee's note and the key into my pocket. Dad was downstairs waiting for me.

"I thought you'd be up earlier," he said. He handed me a granola bar, and I followed him out to the car. "Lewis called at eight-thirty this morning. What's going on? You boys have big plans for the day?"

"Not so much," I said. "Mostly jumping on the mattresses and stuff."

For the whole trip to Lewis's, Dad kept clearing his throat like he was going to say something. We were almost there before he finally spoke.

"I don't want you to feel bad about this whole alien business," he said. "If anyone teases you, I want you to come talk to me. I know it's not easy. Sometimes these kinds of things take time to resolve." He sighed. "And other times, they just stay a mystery." He seemed sad. He thought it was over, but it wasn't. It was hard not to say anything about the alien hunters or Mr. Lee, but I couldn't.

Instead I said, "Don't worry, Dad. It's OK. I bet someone will find out something soon."

For the rest of the ride, I forced myself to be quiet, but it wasn't easy. I had to grind my teeth so I wouldn't talk about it.

When we finally got to the motel, I jumped out of the car and ran straight to the clubhouse.

Nobody was outside, so I climbed up the boxes and peeked in the window. Lewis and Red were sitting at the far side of the room with their backs to the window. I smiled. They were in a perfect position for a surprise attack. I got myself ready and then jumped.

"YYAAHHHH!!" I yelled as loud as I could. I'm sure they were scared, but I couldn't tell because I was rolling around in the pillows in pain. A cannonball is a great idea for water, but not such a great idea when you are landing in pillows.

WHAT I SHOULD <u>NOT</u> HAVE DONE

ME

PERFECT
CANNONBALL
FORM

JUMP
FROM THE
WINDOW

Lewis jumped up and ran over to me. "What did you do that for?" he shouted.

"Don't yell at him! He's hurt," said Red.

"I'm fine," I whimpered. I rolled around some more until the pain dulled and finally went away.

"I wish I'd seen that," said Red.

"Me too," said Lewis, but he still looked kind of mad.

Lewis put his hands on his waist and looked serious. "We've got some things to talk about."

"The alien hunters are bozos," interrupted Red.

Lewis glared at him. "Why do you always do that? Just when I'm about to say something, you jump in and say it first!" Red looked at the ground.

Lewis scowled. "That's not good enough. Get us some snacks, and then maybe I'll forgive you."

Red nodded, dropped to all fours, and disappeared out the dog door.

Lewis watched him go, and then looked back at me. "The alien hunters are bozos," he said.

For the next five minutes, Lewis told me all about the alien hunters. It was easy to see why he was grumpy. I would have been too, but I had a key and a note in my pocket, and that changed everything.

THEY REALLY WERE BOZOS! WHEN THEY WERE NOT HUNTING ALIENS, THEY WORKED AS CLOWNS FOR BIRTHDAY PARTIES.

The Mystery

It didn't take long to tell Lewis about Mr. Lee, the note, and the key. It was a relief to finally tell someone. There were a lot of strange things about it, and even though we tried, Lewis and I couldn't figure them out.

The Strange Things

How did Mr. Lee know about the alien before it was even in the paper? His letter had come two days ago. He'd sent it the day it happened.

- Why did we have to sneak into his garage with a key?
- Why was he worried about us being followed?
- What was he going to tell us?

"I'm back!" shouted Red. He jumped down and landed in front of us. "Here," he said. He held out a bag of strange-looking blobs. "They're muffins. Sage made them."

"Try one," said Lewis. He made a face. "See, I told you—seeds." He pointed to the lumps.

"No thanks," I said. I took a step back.

"They look weird, but they taste OK," said Red. He picked one up and bit into it.

I waved my hand in front of me. "No thanks. I would, but I ate right before I came over. Seriously, I'm not hungry."

"I don't blame you," said Lewis. "If I were you, I

wouldn't eat one either." He grabbed a muffin and took a bite.

I was confused. "How come you're eating it then?"

Lewis mumbled something, but his mouth was full, so it was hard to understand. It sounded like "I'm not you."

STRANGE, LUMPY BLOBS

We spent the whole rest of the morning in the clubhouse. Lewis didn't want to go outside in case the alien hunters were there. That was OK with me. Mostly I was glad that I hadn't studied a bunch of big, impressive words for nothing.

"Do you think Mr. Lee is an alien hunter? But a secret one, so no one knows about it?" Lewis asked. I could tell he was thinking about getting on TV again.

"Maybe," I said, but it was hard to imagine. Mr. Lee had a cane and walked pretty slow. I wondered what kind of alien he'd be able to catch.

Finally it was time to go to meet Mr. Lee. Lewis called Red over and told him that he had to help us by keeping a big secret.

"If Sage asks where we are, tell her we went to do alien research, but don't say it was at the library."

Red nodded.

"Do you promise?" asked Lewis. He made Red hold his hand over his heart.

"OK," said Red. "I promise." He seemed happy to have a secret to keep.

Lewis and I left him in the clubhouse and snuck around the front of the motel.

"Why did you tell him not to say the library?" I asked.

"Because he can't keep a secret," said Lewis. "So if anyone asks him, he'll say the library. It's perfect. Who gets in trouble for going to the library?"

"Genius!" I said, and it was, but at the same time I could think of one person who'd get in trouble. It wasn't a good thought.

FIRST KID IN THE WORLD TO GET IN TROUBLE FOR GOING TO THE LIBRARY

There were only two ways back to my street and Mr. Lee's house—the main road or the path through the woods. Lewis and I both picked the road. There was a greater chance of us being seen, but if we got caught, we wanted it to be by our parents, not the alien.

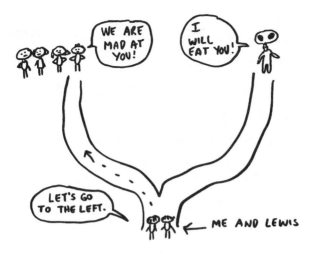

We tried to be fast, but we got to Mr. Lee's house five minutes late.

"We should have left earlier," I said.

Lewis looked at his watch and changed the time to two o'clock. "Now we're perfect," he said.

I pulled the key out of my pocket and held it up.

Lewis seemed a little nervous. "Why can't we just knock on the door?"

"I don't know," I said. "Maybe he's busy."

"Or maybe he's tied up and can't come to the door," said Lewis. "I think we should take some weapons just in case."

I nodded. That was a good idea. We looked around the yard, but there wasn't much to choose from.

"Here," said Lewis. He handed me a tiny shovel. "If someone attacks us, hit their nose, and then I'll trip them with this rake." It was nice that Lewis had the attack all planned out, but I would have felt better with the rake.

Mr. Lee's Garage

I didn't feel ready, but there was nothing else to do except go forward. I put the key into the lock and turned it. It clicked open.

"This feels like a movie," I said.

"Except it's not," whispered Lewis. "It's real, and who knows what's on the other side of that door."

We held our weapons out in front of us and slowly pushed the door open. It was dark inside, and it took a few seconds for my eyes to adjust. There was a light on, but it was near the back of the garage. Slowly, I took a step forward. Lewis bumped into me from behind.

"Stop pushing!" I hissed.

"Well, I can't see anything. You're in the way," he complained.

I took a step to the right so Lewis could stand next to me. Now I could see better. I looked around.

"It's messy!" I whispered. There were chairs and tables and junk piled everywhere.

"What is all this stuff for?" asked Lewis.

"Mr. Lee fixes furniture," I whispered.

"Well, he's got a lot of fixing to do," said Lewis. "This place is a disaster."

Just then, something moved behind us. A second later, the door slammed shut, and the garage was flooded with light.

"AAAHHH!!" I covered my eyes. It was a blinding brightness.

"What the . . . !" shouted Lewis, but a voice interrupted him.

"What are you doing with my wife's tools? I didn't ask you here to garden." It was Mr. Lee's voice.

I moved my hands from my face, and dropped the shovel. Mr. Lee moved his head back and forth, studying us.

"Hi, Mr. Lee." I waved. It was a dumb thing to do, but I was nervous.

"So, you must be Lewis," said Mr. Lee. He stared at Lewis. Lewis nodded and handed him the rake. "Well, you look smart. Are you smart?"

I didn't know if this was a test or not, so when Lewis nodded, I nodded too.

Mr. Lee flashed me a smile, took a step forward, and said, "Follow me and don't touch anything." He leaned the rake next to a chair and headed toward the back of the garage. There was a tiny cleared pathway. We followed.

"I'm not scared," whispered Lewis. "Are you?"

"No," I answered, but it was a lie, because even though I knew Mr. Lee, I was still feeling nervous. It was the kind of nervous that made me wish I still had the shovel.

NOT KNOWING WHAT'S NEXT.

EVERYTHING IS STRANGE.

READY OR NOT, IT'S HAPPENING.

VERY FAST-BEATING HEART.

OH NO! —THE THOUGHT IN MY HEAD.

UNCOMFORTABLE AND SCARED.

SWEATY HANDS.

When Mr. Lee got to the back of the garage, he pushed some of the shelves to the side and disappeared behind them. There was something different about him. It took me a few seconds of thinking to figure it out, but then I got it. It was his walk. His limp was gone, and he wasn't using his cane. I wanted to ask him about it, but he stayed behind the shelves and didn't come back out. Was he looking for something? Lewis and I waited, not saying anything. It seemed like forever.

"Boys! Come!" It was Mr. Lee's voice, but he sounded far away, not like he was just behind the shelves.

"Where'd he go?" asked Lewis.

I shrugged and made a guess. "Outside? Maybe he's got a dog door like you do?"

Lewis and I walked around the shelves to see, but instead of a dog door, there was a skinny set of stairs leading straight underground. Lewis pushed past me.

"Cool! Come on," he said.

I saw Lewis disappear into the dark, and then slowly I followed him down.

DEEP, DARK, DANGEROUS.

OMINOUS.

WHERE DOES IT GO?

NOWHERE GOOD.

The Surprise at the Bottom of the Stairs

I was expecting the space under the garage to be dark and dirty, kind of like a cellar, and I was right—it was. Now I was definitely scared. This was the kind of place where farmers kept their root vegetables or killers murdered people. Could someone who gave you popcorn every year be a killer? I hoped not.

Lewis was in front of me, so it was hard to see. I squeezed in beside him. Now that I could see everything, it didn't look so bad. We were standing in some kind of small workroom. There were stacks of chairs in one corner and wood piled high in another. Straight in front of us was a large workbench.

"This is where I fix my furniture," said Mr. Lee.

"Oh," said Lewis. There wasn't much else to say, so I nodded.

This wasn't turning out to be as dangerous as I thought it would. What did any of this have to do with the alien? Maybe nothing. Maybe Mr. Lee was crazy. I studied him, but I couldn't tell. He looked the same as he always did, but then I remembered the cane.

"Mr. Lee, how come you don't need your cane anymore?"

He looked at me and brushed his chin with his fingers. "Oh, you noticed. Very good, very good. It's part of my disguise, but we don't have time for that. Before we go any further, you must both promise that I can trust you." Mr. Lee looked back and forth between us. "If not, there could be trouble."

"What kind of trouble?" asked Lewis.

"The bad kind!" answered Mr. Lee.

Lewis waited for a second, and then he nodded. When Mr. Lee looked at me, I did the same. I tried to look calm like Lewis, but inside I was anxious, excited, and scared, all at once. It was hard to think straight.

"OK," said Mr. Lee. "Follow me."

"How?" I mumbled. The room was tiny. There wasn't anywhere to go. I moved to the side so

Mr. Lee could get past me and go back up the stairs, but instead he stepped toward the workbench, grabbed a handle on the front, and gave it two quick turns. Instantly, the stack of chairs disappeared into the wall, and in their place was a long, bright hallway. There wasn't a mirror nearby, but I knew exactly what my face looked like. It looked the same as Lewis's.

The Surprise at the End of the Hall

We followed Mr. Lee down the hall. It was hard to believe that all this was under his garage. At the end of the hallway was another door. What did it lead to? Another space?

Lewis was ahead of me. He was going to find

out first. But as soon as the door opened, he stopped moving.

"It's him," said Lewis. His voice was raspy, barely above a whisper. He took a step back, pushing against me. Instantly the hair on my arms tingled, and my heart started racing. I didn't want to look, but at the same time I wanted to know. What was he seeing?

"Who's him?" I whispered.

Lewis moved to the side, and there in front of us was the alien. He was huge. I opened my mouth to scream, but I couldn't make a sound.

Mr. Lee was standing next to it. Was the alien controlling him? Mr. Lee reached over and tapped the alien. Lewis ducked and I cringed, but nothing happened. The alien didn't move—not even a twitch.

"It's a robot," said Mr. Lee. He patted the alien's arm. "It's not real."

Lewis straightened up and took a step forward.

"Yes, yes," said Mr. Lee. He motioned for Lewis to come closer. "You can touch it."

My head felt like it was about to explode, and then everything went dark.

What Happened Next?

Someone was patting me on the head and saying my name. I opened my eyes. It was Mr. Lee. He was leaning over me, staring straight into my face. What had happened? Why was I lying on the floor?

"Oh good. You're OK," said Mr. Lee. He helped me sit up.

"You fainted," said Lewis. He was next to me with a plastic cup. "I was going to throw this water at you, but you can drink it instead." He handed me the cup.

I took a sip of water and looked around. No, it wasn't a dream. I really was sitting in some kind of giant underground hideout, and there, standing in the middle of it all, was the alien.

"It feels sort of slimy," said Lewis. He pointed to it.

Mr. Lee stood up. "I make costumes for movies. Mostly monsters and fantasy creatures."

I gulped down the rest of the water. It was hard to believe my eyes. Everywhere I looked, there were weird, creepy creatures. It was like characters from your worst nightmares, all staring at you at the same time.

"Time to get up," said Mr. Lee. He held my arm, and

I stumbled to my feet. Mr. Lee's words and the images from my eyes were swirling in my head like a giant tornado. It took a few seconds, but slowly they began to fit together. I looked around for Lewis. He was standing next to the alien.

"Touch it," he said. He gave it a pretend punch in the gut.

I walked over and poked it. He was right. It was slimy—it felt cold but sort of alive. I wiped my hand on my pants. Maybe it was only a robot, but it was still creepy.

LEWIS TOUCHING
THE ALIEN

What Mr. Lee Had to Do

I don't know if Mr. Lee was expecting it, but if you scare people in the woods with an alien robot, you're going to have to answer a lot of questions. Both Lewis and I had a bunch of them.

OUR QUESTIONS

1) Why did you have the robot in the woods?
2) Did you know we were in the tree?
3) Why did you take our tortilla chips?
4) Why do you need a disguise?
5) Does Mrs. Lee know about this secret workshop?
6) Do you have a bear suit?
7) Are you famous?
8) Are you going to tell everyone about the robot?

Most of Mr. Lee's answers were kind of a surprise, especially the last one.

MR. LEE'S ANSWERS

1) I was testing the robot to see how well it would work.

2) Yes, I saw you in the tree because the robot has cameras in its eyes.
3) I don't like littering, especially in the woods. But I didn't eat them.
4) I don't want people to know who I really am.
5) Of course my wife knows about this space — she's my wife.
6) No, I don't make animal costumes.
7) Yes, with certain people. That is why I have to keep my workshop a secret. If I had fans coming here bothering me, I'd never get anything done. I like being private.
8) No. If I did that, everything would be ruined. I might even have to move.

My secret favorite answer was number six. It made me smile. I knew Marcus was wrong!

The Studio

After the questions, Mr. Lee gave us a fast tour of his workshop. There were models and creatures everywhere, and piles and piles of plans and drawings. I couldn't read what anything said because it was all written in some sort of weird language. Mr. Lee said it was a special design language that movie designers used, and that it was really hard to learn. Mr. Lee was just like his house—regular on the outside, but super amazing on the inside.

MR. LEE

HARD TO KNOW
HOW COOL HE IS
BY JUST LOOKING
AT THE OUTSIDE
OF HIM

Lewis and I didn't recognize any of the creatures from the movies we'd seen, but Mr. Lee said that was probably because he mostly made models and robots for movies in other countries.

After the tour, Mr. Lee brought out chips and some water, and we all sat around a table in the back of the workshop. There was a big door behind us. I thought it might lead to another room, but Mr. Lee said it was an elevator so he could get his models out of the workshop.

"Can we go out that way?" I asked.

"Yeah, that would be super cool," said Lewis.

Mr. Lee shook his head. "No, it's broken."

Lewis and I both wanted to talk about the elevator some more, but Mr. Lee said, "Forget about the elevator. Have more chips."

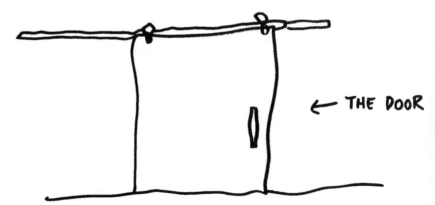

← THE DOOR

Lewis and I were inhaling the chips like we hadn't eaten in days. It must have been all the excitement.

THUMP. THUMP.

We stopped chewing. The sound had come from behind the big door. Something was in there.

"What was that?" asked Lewis.

"What? I didn't hear anything," said Mr. Lee.

"In there." I pointed to the door.

Mr. Lee looked at the door and shrugged. "Probably just the elevator gears," he said. "They're slipping. I told you—it's broken."

Lewis seemed fine with that. He turned, stuck his hand back in the bag, and pulled out a chip. I wasn't so sure. I kept my eye on the door, just in case.

Another Surprise

Some surprises are good. Some are not. Mr. Lee's next surprise was the worst kind—unexpected and impossible.

And he told it to us right when I was in the middle of eating a chip. Mr. Lee said, "I want you boys to tell everyone that you made a mistake about the alien. I want you to help me keep my business here undercover. Maybe you could say you made a mistake and saw a coyote or some other animal instead."

I was so surprised I almost choked. I coughed and spit my chip across the table. It landed in front of Mr. Lee. He stared at it, made a face, and then flicked it off with his finger.

I leaned forward. "We can't do that! It's impossible!" And instantly my brain thought of a million reasons why.

It was hard to look at Mr. Lee's face and say no, so I stared at the chip bag instead. That's when I noticed they were the same kind of chips that

Mom bought—less salt and sort of healthy. It made me wonder.

I pointed to the bag. "Where'd you get those?"

"They're yours from under the tree," said Mr. Lee. He motioned toward the robot.

"The robot carried them?" asked Lewis. "Cool." He leaned in, grabbed another chip, and saluted the robot. I looked over at it.

Sure, it was only a robot, but I didn't trust it.

CREEPY VIBES

Helping Mr. Lee

"I don't know," said Lewis. "We can't really say we didn't see an alien when we already said we saw an alien. I mean, why would we do that? You know, go to all that trouble."

"Maybe I could trade you something," said Mr. Lee. "Something special."

"No way. Impossible," I said. "There's nothing that special."

"Except really cool Halloween costumes," said Lewis. "Those would be special." He looked over at me and smiled. "Awesome, right?"

"No!" I whispered. "Not awesome!"

"OK," said Mr. Lee. "I'll do it. I don't like Halloween, but I'll do it!"

"No!" I stood up. "No deal! We don't want a deal." But both Mr. Lee and Lewis ignored me.

"Why do you hate Halloween?" asked Lewis. "You like costumes."

"I like GOOD costumes," said Mr. Lee. "Not cheap costumes. Bad costumes give me a headache. It's painful."

Lewis shrugged.

ME AS DRACULA ZOMBIE TWO YEARS AGO—I THOUGHT I LOOKED PRETTY GOOD.

BAD GHOST   BAD FRANKENSTEIN

I kicked Lewis under the table a bunch of times until he paid attention to me.

"Oww!" He scowled for a second, and then said, "OK. OK, fine." I let out a sigh. Finally he was listening.

Lewis held up his hand. "Morgan has one more thing for the deal."

"Wait!" What was he talking about?

"Don't worry, I got this." Lewis smiled at me, and then looked back at Mr. Lee.

"He wants you to turn on the alien robot so we can see it working again."

Mr. Lee looked relieved. "Oh, I can do that. I thought you were going to ask for something hard."

I punched Lewis in the arm. "I don't want that!"

"You will when you see it," said Lewis. "It's going to be worth it!" He rubbed his arm and mouthed a silent *OW,* but he wasn't hurt. I should have hit him harder.

Lewis was right. Watching the alien come to life was awesome, but it didn't change the other things. I was still mad.

ALIEN SWINGING A
CHAIR AROUND

IT WAS
SUPER STRONG.

What Lewis Did

After the alien show, Mr. Lee said it was time to leave. Lewis was disappointed, but I was ready to leave. As soon as we were out of sight of Mr. Lee's garage, I exploded. I couldn't keep my words inside anymore.

YOU'VE RUINED MY LIFE!
THAT WAS THE WORST DEAL
EVER!
NOW I HAVE TO LIE AND SAY
I DIDN'T SEE WHAT I
REALLY SAW. PEOPLE ARE
GOING TO BE MAD!
REALLY MAD!
AND YOU DON'T KNOW HOW
MAD MY MOM CAN GET.
SHE CAN BE EVEN
SCARIER THAN THAT ALIEN!
AND SHE'S GOING TO BE
MAD FOREVER!

Lewis looked at the ground. He shuffled his feet. "You were right," he said. "The alien had two legs."

WHAT? That was supposed to fix this? Was he nuts?

Lewis turned to me and pleaded, "We can do this! And we won't lie about seeing the alien. I'll figure out another way, I promise. We have to help Mr. Lee. He needs us—plus don't you want an excellent costume?"

I didn't answer. Of course I wanted an excellent costume, but more than that I wanted to NOT be in trouble. That was number one.

"You'll see," said Lewis. "All we have to do is make everyone forget about the alien."

I didn't bother to nod. We were doomed.

The Worst Luck

When we got back to Lewis's house, Red was around back by the shed. He was doing flips onto the mattresses. At first we thought he was alone, but then we noticed a man watching him.

"They're home!" shouted Red. He pointed at us, jumped off the mattress, and ran over.

"There's a scientist guy here, and he wants to talk to you about the alien," said Red. "Mom said it was OK, and I've been showing him my flips while we waited for you." He was out of breath, but excited. "Isn't that great? He'll probably make you famous."

"OH NO!" I covered my mouth with my hands.

"I'll do the talking," said Lewis. I didn't argue. I was a terrible liar.

"Hi there, boys," said the man. "Red and I have been talking."

Red smiled at the man, and then us.

"So, you boys saw something. I'd like to hear about it." The man reached into his pocket and pulled out our newspaper article, a notebook, a pen, and three business cards. He handed one to each of us. "I'm Mr. Holland."

THE VINCENT HOLLAND CENTER
FOR SUPERNATURAL RESEARCH

VINCENT HOLLAND
HEAD STAFF RESEARCHER

555- ~~~ - ~~~ ~~

Mr. Holland opened his notebook and looked up, waiting for us to talk.

I glanced over at Lewis. He was quiet. I guess he didn't have any big ideas.

"They saw an alien," said Red. "It was in the woods." Red was trying to help us.

"Is that true?" asked Mr. Holland. "Did you see something like that?" He looked down at the newspaper article. "It says here that you saw more than one, and look, you even drew pictures."

"That was a mistake," said Lewis. "We only saw one. But—"

I interrupted him. "But maybe it wasn't an alien. It was kind of hard to tell, because we were really high up in the tree."

"Yeah," said Lewis. "It could have been something else."

"Something else, like what?" asked Mr. Holland. "A squirrel, a dog, a bear?"

"But you said it had three legs!" cried Red. He had no idea what was going on, and was totally confused.

"No, two legs," said Lewis. "I found out I was wrong—" and then he stopped.

"Found out how?" asked Mr. Holland. "Is this new information?" He wrote something down in his notebook.

"No. I just remembered I was wrong," said Lewis. "About the legs."

I stared at the ground. This wasn't going well.

Mr. Holland looked at me, and then back at Lewis. "Sometimes a bear can stand on two legs. Could it have been a bear? You know, there was a bear around here a while ago. Maybe it came back?"

I looked over at Lewis. This was our chance. We could say it was a bear.

"NO! It wasn't a bear!" said Red. He glared at Lewis. "You told me it was an alien, and that it ran away on three legs. I mean, two."

"Alien ran away on two legs," repeated Mr. Holland, and he wrote that down.

"We're not sure about the alien part," said Lewis.

"OK," said Mr. Holland. "So it was an unidentifiable creature, but it ran away on two legs." He looked at us. I felt like he could tell we were lying. I studied the ground and shuffled my feet.

"Yeah," said Lewis. "A running creature."

"Hmm," said Mr. Holland.

This was not good. Any second now, we were going to be in huge trouble. I could feel it.

UGH, THE END IS NEAR!

What Mr. Holland Said That Was a Complete Surprise

"Could it have been a Sasquatch, a Bigfoot?" asked Mr. Holland. "Do you boys know what that is?"

"Is it like a yeti, but instead of living in snow, it lives in the forest?" asked Lewis.

"Sort of," said Mr. Holland. "But the yeti lives in the Himalayas. The Sasquatch is the creature that lives here in the Pacific Northwest. There've been some sightings down the coast from here, so when I heard about your alien story, it was the first

155

thing I thought of." He clapped his hands together and held them in front of his chest. "To find proof of the Sasquatch is a life goal of mine." He tapped his chest and smiled at us.

Lewis was watching me. I nodded, just a little bit, just for him. This was it! Our ticket out of trouble, and it had a giant Sasquatch printed right on the front of it.

The Start of the New Idea

Lewis took a deep breath and said, "It could have been a Sasquatch, right?"

Everyone was looking at me, so I mumbled, "Maybe."

"What exactly does a Sasquatch look like?" asked Lewis.

Mr. Holland pulled a folded piece of paper from his pocket. He handed it to Lewis. It was a colored drawing of a Sasquatch, and it looked nothing like the alien. I didn't say anything, but my brain was busy thinking. I had two main thoughts.

"Looks kind of familiar," said Lewis. He handed the paper back to Mr. Holland. "That could have been it."

Now it was my turn to help out. "Yeah, I'm really

into aliens, so maybe by accident I made the creature look more like an alien than a Sasquatch. I bet if we drew it again, it would turn out better."

There! I had done exactly what I said I wasn't going to do. I'd lied.

Mr. Holland tapped his pen on his pad of paper. "I know how that is. Sometimes a brain can add things that the eyes didn't see, especially if the brain really wanted to see it. I've been waiting eleven years to see a Sasquatch. If I saw an alien, I'd probably do the opposite. I'd turn it into a Sasquatch."

"That would be crazy," said Lewis.

"Yes, it would," said Mr. Holland, and we all started laughing. This whole thing was working out a lot better than I'd imagined. The only person who wasn't happy was Red. He was scowling, but there was nothing I could do about that.

What Happened Next

"Are you a real scientist?" asked Lewis.

Mr. Holland coughed and looked around. "Well, almost a scientist. I don't have a degree, but I know as much as a scientist does, and you can't really get a degree in Sasquatches. It's something you have to learn yourself because—"

"Do you want to see where it happened?" interrupted Red. He was over being grumpy. "We could take you there tomorrow."

"We could?" Both Lewis and I said it at the same time.

"That would be perfect!" said Mr. Holland. "But I can't go tomorrow. How about Monday, at one o'clock?" He didn't wait for an answer. "Sometimes they come back, if they really like an area. Maybe there'll be signs of it—broken branches, crushed leaves, a footprint. It would be great to get some proof that they're in the area."

"What kind of proof?" asked Lewis. "Like a photo?"

"Well, that would really change my life," said Mr. Holland.

"Oh," said Lewis, and then he smiled. I knew that smile—Lewis had a plan.

After the man left, Lewis sent Red to get some snacks. "This time you have to eat whatever Red brings back," he said, "or he'll get suspicious. He'll know we just ask for snacks to get rid of him."

I started to protest, but then agreed. I just hoped it wasn't going to be muffins.

Lewis's Plan

FIRST WE MAKE A SASQUATCH COSTUME.

THEN WE PUT IT ON AND TAKE A PHOTO IN THE WOODS.

FINALLY WE SHOW IT TO MR. HOLLAND.

AND THAT MEANS WE GET OUR COSTUMES FROM MR. LEE.

What Was Wrong with Lewis's Plan?

EVERYTHING!

I had to change Lewis's mind. "We can't make a fake Sasquatch. First, we don't know how to, and second, we have only three days to do it, and third, he's an expert. He'll totally be able to tell our Sasquatch isn't real."

Lewis shook his head. "What's the one thing we needed that we didn't have when we saw the alien?"

I shrugged. "A weapon?"

"NO! A PHOTO!" shouted Lewis. "And that's because a photo would have changed everything. So we don't need to show him a Sasquatch. We just need a picture of a Sasquatch. We make a fake Sasquatch, take a picture of it, and we're done. It'll be proof, and after that, everyone will forget all about the alien. They'll be excited about the Sasquatch and just think we made a mistake."

Lewis pulled out Mr. Holland's card and studied it. "All we have to do is show Mr. Holland the photo. It fixes Mr. Lee's problem, gets us super-great Halloween costumes, and doesn't get you into

trouble." Lewis was happy with
himself. He jogged over to the
pile of mattresses, jumped,
and landed in the middle with
his arms spread wide.

I walked over to him. I was
finished arguing.

"I want my costume to be a dragon," said Lewis.
"With real smoke coming out. Do you think he can
do that?" He sat up. "Make real smoke come out?"
And then he smiled. "Out of both ends!"

I thought about it for a second, and then shook
my head. Lewis was getting distracted. This
Sasquatch thing was important. We had to figure it
out. I had a lot of questions.

My Questions

1) Do we really need a photo?
2) Why can't Mr. Lee make the Sasquatch costume?
3) Don't you think there was something about Mr. Lee that was strange?
4) Do you think we can trust him?

Lewis was Mr. Positive. He had an answer for everything.

I sat next to Lewis and we talked more about Mr. Lee, but Lewis wasn't like me. He wasn't suspicious. He wasn't excited that Mr. Lee was famous. His brain could think about only one thing— getting his dragon costume.

After a while, I gave up arguing with him about the plan. Lewis's idea was probably not going to work, but it was all we had. I couldn't tell Dad that I'd made up the alien story. A switch was the only way to solve everything. Maybe Dad would believe a mistake.

When Red showed up with the snacks, I felt sick.

Not much happened the rest of the afternoon, and for the first time since meeting Lewis, I was glad when Dad picked me up to go home. As soon as Dad pulled into Lewis's driveway, I ran to the car.

"Don't forget to come early," yelled Lewis.

I waved and we were gone. Maybe I'd feel better about stuff tomorrow. I was pretty sure of one thing—I wasn't going to feel any worse.

The Good Things

The day started out OK enough. When I got up, Betty was already gone. "Over to a friend's house," said Mom. It was nice to eat breakfast without the sweater hanging around. That thing could really take your appetite away. After breakfast, Mom asked if Lewis was coming over.

"No. Can you drive me to his house?" I asked.

She sighed and picked up her car keys. I knew what she was thinking. She wanted us to hang out at our house, but there was no way that was going to happen. Not when we were trying to be sneaky. Mom's like one of those spy drones—she sees everything.

When I got to Lewis's house, he had good news. Red was leaving.

I CAN'T HELP YOU. I'M GOING TO THE STORE WITH SAGE.

Having the day to ourselves was a good thing. It made our plan less complicated.

What Is Easy to Do?

Decide you are going to make a fantastic Sasquatch costume.

What Is the Opposite of Easy to Do?

Make even a slightly good Sasquatch costume.

It probably would have been easier if we had fancy supplies like Mr. Lee, but we didn't. All we had were old pillowcases, cardboard boxes, brown paint, and tons of duct tape. The making part was fun, but when Lewis put it on to test it, I knew we were in trouble.

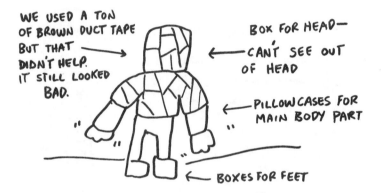

WE USED A TON OF BROWN DUCT TAPE BUT THAT DIDN'T HELP. IT STILL LOOKED BAD.

BOX FOR HEAD— CAN'T SEE OUT OF HEAD

PILLOWCASES FOR MAIN BODY PART

BOXES FOR FEET

"It's hopeless!" I shouted. I was watching Lewis. He was walking around, trying to look like a Sasquatch.

Lewis shook his big head. "You're wrong," he shouted. "If you take a blurry picture, it'll work."

It was a disaster, and he needed to see it. I ran up to him and pulled on his arm.

"Hey," I said. "Let me try it on, and then you can stand back and see how great it looks."

He liked that idea. In two minutes, he was out of the costume, and we were switching places. I pulled everything on, and then jumped around until Lewis yelled at me to stop. It took only about a minute.

"OK," he said. "It's bad."

I took the costume off and dumped it in a heap.

"It looks like a giant brown poop!" said Lewis. He was right. It was funny, but it didn't help. That blob was not going to save my life.

As terrible as it looked, we were stuck with it. We had to make it work!

"It needs to be furry," I said. "Sasquatches have fur."

"Where do we get fur?" asked Lewis.

And then I had the answer. It was crazy, dangerous, and risky, but it was our only choice.

"My house!" I shouted. "Follow me!" And I took off running.

The Mission

Before we went inside, I explained the plan to Lewis.

"Just remember, we have to be quiet," I whispered. I didn't want to get caught. Betty was out with friends, but Mom was home, and she had ears like a superhero.

Lewis and I crept up the stairs to Betty's room. The sweater she'd made for Jason was lying on her desk. When Lewis saw it, he gasped. I was right— it was perfect! It looked exactly like Sasquatch fur. All we needed to do was find Betty's leftover wool. Betty's like me—if she doesn't need something, she shoves it under her bed. Seconds later, I had the bag of wool, and Lewis and I were running to my room. The mission was a success!

What Was Disappointing?

Lewis and I dumped the wool out onto the floor.

Right away I could see that I'd been wrong. This wasn't going to save us.

"It doesn't look as good as the sweater," I said. I picked up a clump and shook it.

"You're right," said Lewis.

We tried sticking it on paper in a bunch of different ways, but everything we did looked bad.

WOOL GLUED ON

WOOL STAPLED ON

WOOL TAPED ON

The Solution

"It's only going to look like fur if we knit it," said Lewis. He grabbed Betty's bag and dug around inside it. "We have to use these." He pulled out two knitting needles and tied a piece of wool to one of them. "Watch me. It's kind of easy once you get started."

I wasn't sure about the easy part, but it was cool to watch Lewis's hands. They moved fast and knew exactly what to do. But then I thought about what we were doing.

"Lewis, stop! We can't do this. It's going to take too long! There's no way we can knit a whole suit."

Lewis ignored me and kept knitting. I grabbed the wool and held it until he stopped pulling back. He dropped the needles.

"You're right," he said. "We're going to need help."

I can't usually read minds, but today was different. I knew exactly what Lewis was thinking.

I had three things to say.

"NO WAY! We can't! She'll kill me!"

"Yes, we have to," said Lewis, and he drew out his plan on a piece of paper.

LEWIS'S PLAN
IF WE STAND IN TALL BUSHES, WE DON'T NEED TO
MAKE A BOTTOM PART FOR THE COSTUME.

MITTIE*

HAT*

MITTIE*

BETTY'S
SWEATER

＊ WHAT WE NEED TO MAKE

What Can Sometimes Happen?

Sometimes, even if you know that something is a
bad idea, you can still agree to do it. Lately, I was
having lots of those times. I should have said,
"Absolutely not! NO CAN DO!" And even though
that's what my brain was thinking, my mouth said,
"OK, but I don't know how we're going to get away
with it."

"We'll figure that out later," said Lewis. He dug around in Betty's bag for some more needles. "Right now I've got to teach you how to knit."

KNOWING HOW TO MOVE THE NEEDLES—

NOT EASY.

IT IS HARDER THAN IT LOOKS.

TAKES A LONG TIME TO DO.

Knitting wasn't as easy as Lewis said it was going to be, or as easy as it looked when he did it. It was surprisingly hard, and every couple of seconds, I did something wrong. Finally, after about twenty minutes, I sort of got the hang of it.

"These are going to be ugly mitties," I said.

Lewis smiled. "That's OK, Sasquatches probably have ugly hands. Plus we'll make the picture sort of blurry, so it won't matter. It'll be perfect."

I kept knitting. Now that I knew what I was doing, it was actually kind of fun.

Knitting

Lewis was good at knitting. After about two hours, he was finished with the hat and working on the second mittie.

He put his needles down. "I'm going to get the sweater and see how it looks with the hat."

I nodded, but didn't look up. I wanted to finish my mittie. Could you get injuries from knitting? It sounded stupid, but my fingers were killing me.

MY HURTING HANDS

The Costume

When Lewis got back with the sweater, I had just finished the mittie. I waved it around in triumph. "Not bad, right?"

Lewis handed me the sweater. "Try it on."

I didn't want to be the one to wear the costume, but I knew I'd be more careful with it than he would. And if we didn't want Betty to find out we'd touched it, being careful was important. I pulled on the sweater and mitties, and then Lewis helped me with the hat. I couldn't see him, but I heard him take a few steps back. It was impossible to see anything with the hat on.

"You're a furry blob," said Lewis. "But a blob who needs eyes."

He was right. We'd forgotten about the eyes.

Lewis tapped me on the shoulder. "Stay still. I'll find something."

I mumbled an OK. It was hard to talk with the hat on—the wool kept getting in my mouth. I'd been right about the sweater—it was itchy. I hoped Lewis was going to be fast. After what seemed like forever, I heard him coming toward me.

"These will work," said Lewis. He grabbed my head and shoved something hard onto the outside of the hat, right by my eyes.

"OW!" I yelled and tried to push him away. "Are you trying to blind me?" I thrashed around, but missed hitting him. I pulled the hat off to see what he'd done.

The eyes weren't great, but they were better than nothing.

HAT WITH EYES

"Where'd you get those?" I asked. They looked kind of familiar.

"I just found them," said Lewis, and then he pointed.

What I Said to Lewis

"YOU KILLED BINKY!!!!!"

BINKY WITHOUT EYES

Lewis apologized a lot, and I could tell that he felt bad, but it was too late. Binky was blind! It was something I would have to forgive him for, but it was not going to be easy.

I tried to be cool about the whole Binky thing, but I wasn't very good at pretending. I knew Lewis could tell I was upset.

After we put Betty's sweater back, and hid the mitties and the hat under the bed, Lewis said he had to go home.

Mom drove him home and I went along for the ride. I thought Mom might be surprised when we found her and asked her to drive Lewis home, but she said she'd heard us come in. I crossed my fingers and hoped that we'd been quiet and that she hadn't heard anything else. A Mom/Betty angry team-up was not something I wanted to experience.

Lewis and I didn't say much on the ride to his house. It was hard to be chatty after what had just happened.

Sunday

Sunday should have been called surprise day because the surprises started even before I woke up. Lewis came over extra early. Mom might have made him go back home, but Dad was the one who answered the door, so he let him come up to my room.

Seeing Lewis's big face staring down at me when I first opened my eyes was a surprise. I screamed, sat up, and smashed him on the chin with my head. It was an accident, but I could tell that he was hurt and upset. He was quiet the whole time I was getting dressed, and usually he's a complete chatterbox. He didn't say anything until we walked downstairs and into the kitchen. And then the first thing he said was about food.

"Can we have cereal?" he asked.

I pulled out the Cheerios and Froot Loops. He pointed to the Froot Loops. I poured out two bowls.

As we were finishing our cereal, Betty came down. She didn't seem surprised to see Lewis. I guess she'd heard him talking. She made herself some toast and sat down with us.

"How's Jason?" asked Lewis. I cringed. He wasn't supposed to ask her about that. He wasn't even supposed to know about it.

"It's too early for boyfriends," complained Betty. "Can we talk about something else?"

"OK," said Lewis. "What's up for today?"

"Why?" asked Betty. "Are you spying on me?"

I held my breath. If she was going to be hanging around the house all day, we were doomed.

Lewis smiled and said, "Maybe."

"Well, you'll have to come to the mall, and then Sophie's house, because I'm going to be gone all day." Betty popped the last bite of toast into her mouth.

"Bummer," said Lewis.

Betty rolled her eyes. "Yah, whatever. I have to get ready." She pushed herself away from the table, put her plate in the dishwasher, and went upstairs.

"Your sister likes me," said Lewis.

"Well, I wouldn't take that as a compliment," I said. "She likes a lot of weird things."

I LIKE PRETEND BOYFRIENDS, KNITTING UGLY SWEATERS, GRAPE JELLY AND CELERY, SHOPPING FOR SOCKS, ANYTHING TO DO WITH PENGUINS, AND LEWIS—HE'S NICE.

Binky Can See!

Lewis and I went up to my room to wait for Betty to leave. As soon we got there, he pulled something out of his pocket and handed it to me. I looked at my hand. Two eyeballs were staring back at me.

"I'm going to fix your friend," he said.

Lewis dug around in his pocket again and pulled out a little tin. He opened it and pulled out a needle and some thread. I didn't know what to say.

"Hand over the Binkster," said Lewis.

"You can sew too?" It was hard to believe.

"Just a little, but I can fix him."

I pulled Binky off my bed and handed him over.

"Where did you get the eyes?" I asked. They had pieces of blue fur around them.

"I just had them," said Lewis. And then he ignored me and sewed new eyes on Binky.

BINKY WITH NEW EYES

The Woods

After Betty left, Lewis and I grabbed the sweater, hat, and mitties, and snuck out of the house. It didn't take long to get to the trail. And it took us no time to get to the tree. When we got there, Lewis stopped and looked up.

"Can you believe how much stuff has happened near this tree?" he asked. I nodded. It was odd.

Lewis pointed to an area off the trail that was thick with bushes.

"If you get in the middle of that big bush over there, it'll be perfect. It's high enough so we won't see your legs. That way all we'll see is the Sasquatch costume."

"I hope there's no poison ivy in there," I said. "Do you know what it looks like?"

"No." Lewis shook his head. "But I'm sure there's none. They wouldn't put a trail next to poison ivy."

I wasn't so sure. "But it's not next to the trail. The trail's over there and—"

"Just go," interrupted Lewis.

"Fine." I grumbled and took a step off the trail. Slowly I picked my way through the weeds and prickles to get to the bush that Lewis had pointed out. Halfway there, I stopped and waved to Lewis. "Hey! I found something! Come look!"

Lewis tried to ignore me, but I called him until he finally trudged over to where I was standing.

"What is it?" he asked.

I pointed to the ground and moved the bushes to the side so he could see.

"It's our hotel sign!" he shouted. "The Stay On Inn sign!" He leaned over and tried to lift it, but it wouldn't budge, not even an inch. "It's too heavy!" he complained.

"How did it get here?" I looked around. It didn't make sense. The path was too narrow for a truck or car, and the sign weighed a ton, much too heavy to carry. It was a mystery.

"I don't know how we'll get it out of here," said Lewis. "I'll have to ask Dave." He hesitated for a minute, and then walked back to the path.

I wanted to go back to the path too, but I couldn't. I continued forward.

What Was Not as Easy as Lewis Said It Was Going to Be

Getting into the middle of the giant, prickly bush was tricky. Every time I moved a branch, my hands got scraped up, and if I didn't move the branches, the rest of me got scraped up, but finally I made it. I waved to Lewis.

"Great! Now put on the costume!" he shouted.

Putting Betty's sweater on was almost impossible. Every single prickly branch wanted to grab hold of it and not let go. It took forever, but finally I had everything on—the sweater, the hat, and the mitties. It was like a torture suit, and I was sweating.

I turned toward Lewis and did my best Sasquatch pose.

"The hat's backward!" shouted Lewis.

"You're kidding!" I moaned, but of course he was right. I lifted my hand to turn the hat, but my mittie got caught on a branch. I tried to pull it loose, but nothing happened. The branch wouldn't let go. I twisted my body to get a better grip, but almost fell. Now the prickles were pulling on the sweater too. It was like trying to move in a giant, sticky spiderweb. No matter what I did, I only got more tangled.

I could hear Lewis talking to me in the distance. "What are you doing? Stop squirming! Wait! Wait! That's a good pose. Got it! OK. We can go."

That was easy for him to say. I pulled on the mittie as hard as I could, but I couldn't break free. My arm was stuck—the branch was pulling one way, and I was pulling the other! And worse, now there was no way to get the sweater off with only one hand. I thrashed my arms in the air, hoping something would break.

"Quit fooling around!" shouted Lewis.

I pulled the hat off with my free hand and glared at him.

He couldn't tell what was wrong. He waved for me to come back to the path.

I stared at the branch that was holding the mittie and yanked with both hands. It was a desperate tug-of-war and a surprise when the branch suddenly let go. The mittie had ripped in two, and the other half was still hanging on the branch. I didn't care. I was free.

"Keep it!" I yelled.

HALF A MITTIE

I walked free of the prickle bush and then pulled off the sweater. It was a slow trudge back to the path.

"What took so long?" asked Lewis. "What . . ."
But then he stopped talking. He was staring at my
hands. "We should go," he said. "I've got to work on
these photos, and you need bandages."

"And infection cream," I said. "And itchy cream."
My hands were killing me, but that wasn't all—my
ankles were suspiciously itchy. I had a feeling I
suddenly knew what poison ivy looks like.

HANDS SCRATCHED UP AND BLEEDING

The Photo

Lewis walked me home. It wasn't the original plan,
but I think he felt bad about my cuts, and I'd done the
same thing for him. The only difference was he didn't
use Mom's trick to keep me distracted. We just pretty
much walked in silence. It was probably smarter,
because by the time we got to my house, he hadn't
made any promises he didn't want to keep.

Lewis left me on the doorstep and turned to go home, but then stopped.

"Do you think it could have been the alien?" he asked.

"What?" What was he talking about?

"That took the sign and dumped it in the woods."

"Why would Mr. Lee do that?" I asked.

"I don't know." Lewis shrugged. "There's just a lot of strange stuff going on. Forget it. It doesn't make sense."

He waved and jogged off, but I didn't forget it. Was Mr. Lee up to something?

What Mom Looked Like When She Saw Me

"I'm OK. I just fell in some prickle bushes." And then I smiled to show her I really was OK.

Mom held my hands and inspected them. "Are you sure you weren't attacked by prickle bushes?"

"Yeah, I kind of was. I got stuck. But I'm fine, just thirsty."

Two seconds later, Betty walked in. The sweater—HER SWEATER—was in my bag! I looked around desperately. I had to get upstairs before she did.

Mom called to Betty before she disappeared. "Betty, get Morgan some apple juice and a cookie." Then she turned back to me. "Now let's clean your scratches."

All I could think about was getting upstairs. I jumped up. "I have to go to the bathroom!"

"I'm sure you can wait a minute or two. Sit down."

"I can't wait!" I hopped up and down. "Remember what happened with the alien?" I pointed to my pants. "It's an emergency!"

Mom shook her head. "OK, go! But don't get blood on the hand towels."

I grabbed my bag and raced upstairs. I could hear Betty complaining in the background. Hopefully, Mom wasn't going to tell her about my alien accident, but there was nothing I could do about that.

I ran into the bathroom, slammed the door, and grabbed Betty's sweater out of the bag. Then I quietly opened the door and snuck across the hall into Betty's room and returned the sweater. The whole thing took only about ten seconds.

Five minutes later, I was bandaged up and eating a cookie. It was kind of hard to hold, but it was chocolate chip, so it was worth the extra effort.

BANDAGED FLIPPER
HAND WITH
COOKIE

The Meeting at Lewis's House

I thought I'd be all healed the next day, but I wasn't. I still had to wear the bandages. At first, Mom was absolutely and positively not going to let me go to Lewis's house, but after I pleaded and whined for about twenty minutes, she finally said yes. It was hard to buckle my seat belt with flipper hands, but I didn't complain. One wrong word and I knew we'd be headed back home.

Mom looked at me in the rearview mirror. "I don't know what you think you're going to be able to do over there, with your hands all bandaged up."

"Just hang out," I answered.

"Well, no jumping off that shed. Don't think I don't know what's going on." She turned around and gave me her mom eye.

"Mom, the road!" I yelled.

She turned back to the road and shook her head. How did she know about the shed? It must have been Dad. So much for keeping a secret!

"It looks like rain," said Mom. "Don't get those bandages wet or I'll have to wrap you up all over again. Do you hear me?"

I mumbled a yes.

Lewis and Red were in the front yard, waiting for me.

"Whoa! What's that?" asked Red. He was looking at my hands.

"Prickle bushes," I said. I waved to Mom, and we watched her drive away.

The second she was gone, I said, "Show me the picture! Is it good?"

"Pretty good," said Red. "But not awesome."

Lewis turned to him. "Can you just let me talk?"

Red nodded and looked down.

"I had to tell him about our Sasquatch thing," said Lewis. "But he promised not to tell, right?"

"Right," said Red. "It's a surprise project for school for ant apology."

"Anthropology," corrected Lewis. He winked at me.

"Got it," I said. It was another genius cover-up.

ANT APOLOGY

I'M SORRY I STEPPED ON YOUR TOE.

ANTHROPOLOGY

IT'S THE STUDY OF HUMANS AND THEIR ANCESTORS.

I COULD BE YOUR ANCESTOR.

The Photo

I don't know what I was expecting, but the photo in Lewis's hand was not it. Even with fur, our Sasquatch looked nothing like Mr. Holland's Sasquatch. It was out of focus and in the bushes like we wanted, but it still looked wrong.

ME PULLING TO GET THE MITTIE
OFF THE BRANCH

"It's too small," I said. "And kind of funny shaped."

"Maybe we could say it was a baby one," suggested Lewis.

"I don't know," I said. "I've never heard of a baby Sasquatch."

"Well, they have to exist," said Lewis. "Everyone starts out as a baby." It was a good point, but I wasn't sure it was going to help.

I held the picture out in front of me and squinted. It looked sort of OK if you had your eyes almost closed.

"We shouldn't show him this until we get to the tree," I said. "It'll be darker in the woods. It'll look better in the dark."

"Good idea," said Lewis. "Hey, Red, how about getting us some snacks for our adventure?"

Red was not excited. "How come I always have to get the snacks?" he complained.

"Do you want to be part of this or not?" said Lewis.

"OK," grumbled Red, and he stomped off.

"He can't come," said Lewis.

"Right," I said. It made sense, but I felt bad for Red. He was going to be disappointed. Maybe if I could find a good stick, I'd make him a slingshot. I'd keep on the lookout. Plus having a project would make me less nervous around Mr. Holland. This whole thing was making my hands and ankles itch again. Mom said it wasn't poison ivy, but whatever it was, it still felt horrible.

Lewis and I waited for Mr. Holland out by the road. He was five minutes early like we were, which was good for us but bad for Red.

As soon as Mr. Holland saw me, he pointed to my hands. "What happened to you?"

"Bush accident," I answered. I liked how that sounded—sort of mysterious and rugged, not embarrassing and clumsy and like what had really happened.

"Should we go?" asked Lewis, and then without waiting for us to say yes or no, he marched off toward the woods.

I jogged to catch up, and Mr. Holland followed behind.

What Mr. Holland Said When He Saw the Tree

"Wow! You boys did a great job marking that tree."

"Thanks," said Lewis. It was a compliment for me, but I let Lewis take it. I was too worried to argue.

Mr. Holland took out his notebook and camera and started looking around. When he went behind the tree, Lewis patted his pocket and raised his eyebrows. He wanted to show the photo. I shook my head. I was having new thoughts about the photo, and they were not good.

Lewis put his hand into his pocket. I grabbed his arm.

"Not now," I whispered.

He nodded. We were safe, at least for a little bit. What I really wanted to do was get the photo away from him and rip it up, but that was impossible.

I looked up at the sky. It was definitely going to rain. If I was lucky, it would start soon and then we'd all have to go home. That was the best I could hope for.

I heard Mr. Holland yelling, "Hey, what's that?"

He pointed in the distance. "That brown thing, over there, on that bush?"

Lewis and I looked to where he was pointing. It took me a second to spot what he was looking at, but when I did, my heart stopped. It was my half-mittie waving in the wind.

"That looks like something," said Mr. Holland. "Maybe fur."

Before either of us could say anything, Mr. Holland left the path and was headed through the weeds straight for the prickle bush.

What Dread Feels Like

YOU ARE SURROUNDED BY THIS

"What should we do?" I whispered.

"You should have let me show the photo!" hissed Lewis. "Now it could—" But he was interrupted by a strange and terrible scream.

"YEEEOOOWWLLLLLLEEEEEEE!"

We looked for Mr. Holland, but he was gone.

"Something got him," whispered Lewis.

We looked around desperately. I don't know what Lewis was thinking, but I was thinking bear.

Then we heard a faint "I'm OK."

We scanned the bushes, and suddenly Mr. Holland's head popped up. He tried to stand but stumbled. He rubbed his forehead with his hands. They were all scratched up. I knew how that felt.

Mr. Holland pointed to his feet. "I tripped and hit my head," he said. "There's something down here." He rubbed his head again, and now I could see a little red spot.

"We should have brought some bandages," said Lewis. "I never—"

"EEIIIAWW! EEIIIAWW!"

"Ssshhhh!" I grabbed Lewis's shoulder. "Did you hear that?"

We listened. It was a strange whistling sound, kind of like a bird, but not a bird. It was something else. The sound made the hairs on my arms stand straight up and my whole body shiver. And then we heard it again. Suddenly there was something moving in the trees over to the left, past Mr. Holland.

Lewis gasped.

We saw it only for a second—a big, brown furry thing, and it wasn't a bear. I choked down the scream that was stuck in my throat.

My brain could think of only one thing, and it was on a constant loop: "Keep quiet and it will go away! Keep quiet and it will go away! Keep quiet and it will go away!" I grabbed the tree next to me, and Lewis and I stood dead still, our eyes scanning the bushes. I hardly wanted to breathe, and then as fast as it had appeared, it was gone.

Finally Lewis spoke. "I don't believe it!" he whispered. "Was that what I think it was?"

I nodded, too stunned to speak.

"UNBELIEVABLE!" said Mr. Holland. He was racing out of the bushes toward us. "Did you boys hear that? That's a Sasquatch's call. I've never heard it before, only been told about it. Made the hairs on the back of my neck stand straight up. Did you hear it?"

"You didn't see it?" asked Lewis. "It was there!" He pointed past where Mr. Holland had fallen.

"You saw it? Again? Both of you?"

We nodded. Mr. Holland turned and quickly scanned the bushes behind him, but it was too late.

"I was looking down," he said. "I tripped on some kind of sign over there." He pointed to where he'd disappeared. "Who throws a sign in the woods? It's not something you expect when you're walking in the bushes." He sighed and wiped a tiny stream of sweat off his forehead before it got to his eye. I thought he might be disappointed, but he was filled with energy.

"I want you boys to show me exactly where it was."

Morgan the Leader

My bandages were perfect for walking through the bushes. I had flippers of protection against the prickles. Lewis and Mr. Holland were not so lucky. Their hands were definitely going to get scratched up. I took the lead—I think they were glad about that. It was easier to follow someone than to go first. It took us about ten minutes to get to the spot where the Sasquatch had stood. I still couldn't believe we'd seen it, an actual Sasquatch. First an alien, and now a Sasquatch. What was next?

I was glad that Lewis was complaining about the prickles. Hopefully all the noise he was making would scare the Sasquatch away if it was still hanging around. Mr. Holland said they were shy creatures. Shy or not, I didn't want to run into it. If Mr. Holland wasn't with us, I would have definitely been walking in the opposite direction.

Discovery

When we got to the Sasquatch spot, Lewis and I waited next to a tree while Mr. Holland looked around. Neither of us wanted to do any extra moving through prickle branches if we didn't have to.

We weren't watching Mr. Holland, so it was a surprise when he screamed. He was down again. We rushed over, but this time he hadn't fallen. He was on the ground examining something.

"It's a footprint," he said. "Look! It's fantastic."
He took out his camera and started taking pictures.

I didn't know that a footprint could be so exciting,
but Mr. Holland said it was very important. He took
photos of it, measured it, and then when
it started to rain, even tried to dig it
out with a stick.

"It'll be gone before I can get back
here with plaster. I want to make a
model of it," said Mr. Holland. Hearing
him talk about models made me
think of Mr. Lee, but that was only
for a second because the next second
Mr. Holland was looking around frantically for another
stick. I could tell Mr. Holland's plan of digging out the
footprint was not going to work, but Lewis and I
helped him anyway. We looked around to find him
new sticks he could use as a shovel.

I don't know why this happens, but sometimes
when you're looking for something, you can't find it.
And then when you stop looking for it, there it is
right in front of you. Maybe that's why I found it. It
was the first stick I picked up, and it was perfect—
my perfect stick.

Red was going to have an amazing slingshot!

BANDAGED HAND
HOLDING THE
PERFECT STICK

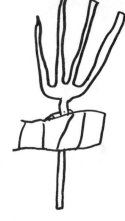

What Happened Next?

A lot of things happened after we saw the Sasquatch. Some were good for me, some were good for me and Lewis, some were good for Lewis's family, and of course Red got a triple slingshot so that was good for him.

What Was Good for Me

Dad was understanding about the whole alien-Sasquatch thing. Once Mr. Holland told everyone about the Sasquatch, Dad just took me to get my eyes checked.

And Dad was right—I needed glasses.

WOW!
I CAN
SEE
BETTER

Another plus was that I finally got to know what the sign above Lewis's door meant.

WHAT IT SAID

WHAT IT WAS SUPPOSED TO SAY

What Was Good for Me and Lewis

We didn't have to show anyone the bad photo of me dressed up as a Sasquatch. In fact, Lewis even let me keep it, which was nice of him and a surprise for me. I think being happy about our Halloween costumes put Lewis in a generous mood. We got our names in the paper again, and this time, a photo too. Mr. Holland was in the photo with us, and that was good because it made it more official. I was glad that he had heard the Sasquatch whistle because I didn't want Lewis and me to be the only witnesses again. School was about to start, and I wanted to be ready for Marcus.

What Was Good for Lewis's Family

Their motel business got busy with customers. People came from all over to try to see the Sasquatch. It was a lot of work, but they finally finished making all the rooms nice. They wanted to get the sign out of the woods, but nobody had any good ideas about how to do it.

LEWIS'S PARENTS—DAVE AND SAGE

What Was Maybe Good or Bad, but We Can't Tell

Yesterday I got a letter in my mailbox. I recognized the handwriting. It was from Mr. Lee.

Dear Morgan and Lewis,
Please use the enclosed key to open my side garage door. Please come at 2 p.m. on Friday. Do not let anyone follow you. I need to talk to you about my Sasquatch.
                    Your Friend,
                    Mr. Lee

This time we are going to be prepared.

GET READY FOR BOOK 2
IN THE SASQUATCH AND ALIEN SERIES!

Super Sasquatch Showdown

THE TRUTH-TELLING WATCH

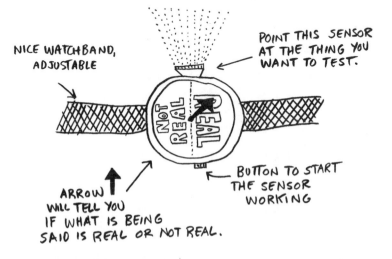

POINT THIS SENSOR
AT THE THING YOU
WANT TO TEST.

NICE WATCHBAND,
ADJUSTABLE

NOT REAL

REAL

BUTTON TO START
THE SENSOR
WORKING

ARROW
WILL TELL YOU
IF WHAT IS BEING
SAID IS REAL OR NOT REAL.

If you had a watch like this, it would be valuable, maybe the most valuable watch in the entire world. A watch like this can tell you if an alien is real or a robot, if Mr. Lee is who he says he is, if a Sasquatch is a friend or foe, and if the world really is about to be taken over by hungry aliens. It would help with a lot of other things, but this watch hasn't been invented yet, so Morgan and Lewis will just have to figure out all these things for themselves.